STAIRS OF THE GODS

THE FALLEN ELVES
BOOK TWO

LEAH R CUTTER

KNOTTED ROAD PRESS

Reviews
It's true. Reviews help me sell more books. If you've enjoyed this story, please consider leaving a review of it on your favorite site.

Come someplace new...
Are you a traveler? Do you enjoy exploring strange new worlds, new cultures, new people?

Sign up for my newsletter and I'll start you on your travels with a free copy of my book, *The Island Sampler.*

http://www.LeahCutter.com/newsletter/

Buy More!
Did you know that you can buy directly from the Knotted Road Press website?

https://www.knottedroadpress.com/shop/

ALSO BY LEAH R CUTTER

Urban/Contemporary Fantasy Series

The Shadow Wars Trilogy

The Raven and the Dancing Tiger

The Guardian Hound

War Among the Crocodiles

The Cassie Stories

Poisoned Pearls

Tainted Waters

Spoiled Harvest

Bloodied Ice

The Witch's Progress

Circle of Air

Circle of Fire

Circle of Water

Circle of Earth

Seattle Trolls

The Changeling Troll

The Princess Troll

The Fairy-Bridge Troll

The Troll-Demon War

The Troll-Human War

The Troll-Troll War

The Clockwork Fairy Kingdom

The Clockwork Fairy Kingdom

The Maker, the Teacher, and the Monster

The Dwarven Wars

The Chronicles of Franklin

Franklin Versus The Popcorn Thief

Franklin Versus The Soul Thief

Franklin Versus The Child Thief

Science Fiction

The Long Run

Project Nemesis

Project Nyx

Project Tisiphone

Project Persephone

War of the Allied Worlds

The Labors of Darius Linard

Huli Intergalactic: Science/Space Fantasy

Origins

The Strawberry Girl

Mysteries

The Purloined Letter Opener

The Tell Tale Heart Pin

Dancer in Darkness

Trophy Hunters

The Alvin Goodfellow Case Files

The Rabbit Mysteries

The Shredded Veil Mysteries

Mystery, Crime, and Mayhem

MAP

Broken Mountains
Wastelands
Forbidden Forest
Gishem Woods
Blasted Plains
Dorwin River
Nyramukz Mountains
Ilburh Territory
Endless Ocean
Tumenzir Desert
Stair Rocks
N

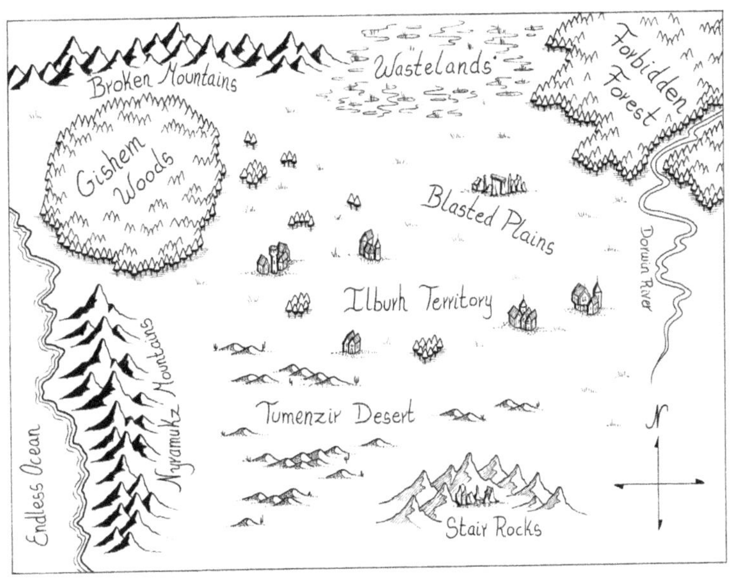

CHAPTER

ONE

Though Tanelith was one of the Egarlorsar, also known as Elves, she spent the day camped in a pine tree, like one of the Meerimec, or Tree People. Using her elven magic, she'd climbed up high up into the tree, then woven herself a small nest to lay in out of the branches.

She was traveling through an uninhabited area, on her way back from the Broken Mountains to Gishem Woods. Keeping herself safe and alive was Tanelith main focus. Anyone going past the tree might not even see her, though she hadn't met any other travelers in the two days she'd been walking across the plain.

She was midway between the foot of the Broken Mountains to the north, and Gishem Woods to the south. It had grown much colder in the two months since the last time she'd crossed this plain, when she'd been heading north, toward the mountains. Even in her much nicer and warmer clothes, chill winds nipped at her, leaving her cheeks chapped and her nostrils raw. Snow had covered the tops of the mountains just the day before, and would soon be smothering the dried grass of the meadow around her.

Tanelith had been lucky that year, and winter had been a month late in coming. However, it was bearing down hard on her

1

now. She needed to get further south, and soon, before traveling grew much more difficult.

Because Tanelith was an elf, one of the Egarlorsar—the Moon People—she could use her magic to walk on top of the snow, at least for a while. But traveling that way was exhausting, plus every time she stopped to camp it would be wet and cold. All she had was a roll to sleep on, not a tent. Though Tanelith could call a lot of magic to her, all that would drain even her.

Tanelith had gone back to traveling at night and sleeping during the day. Moonlight powered her magic, and it had been the full moon just the night before. She'd discovered, though, that even during the dark of the moon her magic was stronger at night than during the day, particularly when the sun was beating down on her.

The opposite was true for the Ilburh, the Humans who worshiped the sun. The Meerimec, also known as the little folk, were strongest when they were in the woods, among the trees. She assumed that the magic of the dwarves—the Gilukkhaz—was most powerful in the mountains, surrounded by stone, though they could perform great magic on the earth as well.

Tanelith stretched out and peered down from her nest, toward the base of the pine currently granting her shelter. What little grass stubbornly sticking up between the dropped needles was drooping and brown. A furry brown rabbit hopped by, looking for a few more tidbits to nibble on before scurrying back to its warm den for the night. Squirrels chittered at her from the other branches. There weren't as many birds in the trees or the plain now, as they'd mostly traveled south for the winter.

Twilight had fallen. The wind swirling the needles blew cold and dry. Clouds covered the moon, but Tanelith could still see fine, as all of the Moon People could. However, the days were growing quickly shorter.

While the Human Ilburh had set calendars, with weeks gathered into months that made no sense to Tanelith, the elves measured their days and years with the waxing and waning of the moon.

The longest night was coming, the time that her people always marked as the start of the new year. Tanelith bitterly regretted that she'd miss all the celebrations. She'd probably be traveling by herself when the new year came in a month or so.

Still, she needed to be on her way. She put her pack on her back, then climbed gracefully down the tree. She used her magic to wipe away the sticky resin of the tree, brushing her hands across the knees of her trousers to do the same.

She would reach Gishem Woods before dawn. At that point, she might have to rest again, changing her schedule around to travel more during the day.

She was on her way to see Loba, the old Meerimec woman who had traveled far and wide in her youth. If anyone knew how to help Tanelith, she would.

Tanelith still felt shock when she thought about the cloud she'd seen—and the city that she knew was hidden inside of it.

Five hundred years before, the gods as well as the Egarlorsar had lived in cities that floated far above the ground of Ithlond. Then, during the War of Betrayal, the cities had supposedly all been shot down, destroyed. Tanelith had grown up in the ruins of the city of Lasirinth on the Blasted Plains.

She'd always been told that none of the cities had survived.

However, the people of the Broken Mountains believed that while all the floating cities had touched ground during the War of Betrayal, some had managed to regain the sky. Those people were still waiting to be rescued, assuming that someday, the floating cities would come and scoop them all up.

Tanelith would bet that the city that floated amongst the clouds would never deliberately travel over the Broken Mountains, possibly because they didn't want to be recognized.

How was she to reach the city? Her magic wouldn't send her flying into the clouds, no matter how much she might wish. She knew there had to be a way. According to the old legends, people from the cities regularly came down to Ithlond, and vice versa.

Loba would surely know how Tanelith could get to the city, or at least be able to point Tanelith toward someone who might know. The old Meerimec had learned much during her travels.

If Loba didn't know, Tanelith did have a second place to search. Old Olin, the shopkeeper who repaired and sold ancient artifacts back in her home village, might have a clue hidden in one of the numerous books he kept. He might even know himself, without needing to look it up.

However, traveling back home was fraught with difficulty. It either meant traveling along the borderland of the Wastelands and the Broken Plains, risking madness and ill magic, or traveling across the lands of the Ilburh, where she would be hunted again.

The slaver Ugmas was still coming after her. In fact, all of the slavers would be. It was a point of honor among them that no slave ever escaped.

They would hunt her to the day she died. Or until she ended the slave trade. Whichever came first.

Was that to be her destiny? To call down another great war between the races and to free her people? She'd never felt like a warrior, had never studied fighting. The Egarlorsar didn't fight, not like the other races.

Everyone blamed the elves for the War of Betrayal. Their pride had been their downfall, at least according to the other races. So the elves didn't fight, didn't have warriors at their beck and call. They'd disarmed themselves.

And now they were being turned into slaves.

As the dusk settled, night winds rose up, blowing harshly as Tanelith ate a little of the soft bread and hard cheese she'd carried with her from the Broken Mountains. Those would be gone in a day or so, as well as the dried berries, though she'd tried to dole those out only a few at a time to make them last. Then she would switch to what Ladriell, the apprentice priestess she'd met in the Broken Mountains, had called a *travel roll*. The dough was first rolled out thin, then layers of lard, dried meat, dried fruit, and spices were spread across it. After rolling the dough up again tightly with the ends pinched closed, it was baked. The dough turned tough, making it difficult to chew. But she just needed a little for any meal, and a roll would last her a long while, weeks more perhaps, particularly in this cold.

Hopefully she would have found Loba before too long and could replenish her food supply.

Tanelith spent a few more moments looking across the open field just past the trees. Even without the moon, it still spread out like a gray sea, the tops of the grass waving in the winds. No one else was in sight. She couldn't hear the clanking of chains that a slave cart carried. Just the quiet whispering of the wind, carrying the smell of more snow.

Time to get moving. This was only the first part of what she knew would become a long, long journey.

She took off, using the power of the moon to aid her speed, racing across the plain. Though her situation wasn't good—hunted by slavers, seeking what might turn out to be impossible to find—she still found her heart light as she ran.

At least for now.

CHAPTER

TWO

The trees of Gishem Woods loomed darkly above Tanelith's head. Though Tanelith could see well enough despite the cloud-covered sky, she couldn't peer between the gigantic trunks. It would take five men with their arms outstretched to reach around the trunk of just one of the trees. Giant roots, each bigger around than her thigh, grew out from the base of each tree, overlapping the roots of its neighbors and blocking the path.

In the daylight, the bark of those huge trees would be a blood-red color. Legend had it that each one contained a single drop of the blood of the great Meerimec hero Heobo.

Loba had called these trees the guardians, and claimed that they were more aware than the rest of the woods. Tanelith believed it. She'd seen that for herself. The first time she'd visited them, they'd turned her around. It wasn't until she'd pleaded with them that they'd made a path for her.

This time, before Tanelith even tried to cross the border and go into the woods, she walked up to one of the trees and put her hand on the rough bark.

"I'm here to see Loba," she announced. "I seek her aid."

Was it her imagination that a wind suddenly rustled the branches of the outer trees?

No, there was definitely a wind. It had shifted around and was now blowing against her back.

She looked over her shoulder for a moment, wondering where the wind had come from.

When she looked forward again, she could suddenly see in past the trunks of the outer ring of trees. There wasn't a path necessarily—she'd still have to be walking past roots all the time, being careful of where she stepped. However, the wide opening meant that it would be a lot easier to travel.

A sudden gust of wind pushed at her back again.

Did the trees want her to hurry?

"Is there something wrong with Loba?" Tanelith asked.

The trees didn't deign to speak with her. She had this sense of urgency, though.

"Thank you for letting me travel through you," Tanelith added before she took that final step under the trees.

The stillness struck her first. It was as if the grand trunks muted all sounds. As dawn approached, she heard chickadees chirping and the clicking of juncos, even the raucous cry of a jay. All the sounds still seemed faint and far away, though.

The air carried the sweet smell of cedar, as well as a biting cold. The guardian trees were all a type of pine, though not one she'd ever seen before. She shivered as she hurried along. She wouldn't start a fire as she traveled through the woods. Though the trees might understand, they also might not. She would just have to use more of her magic to keep herself warm, though she would miss heating water for tea.

Tanelith traveled as far as she could that morning before she finally had reached the end of her reserves and took a nap, snoozing at the base of one of the big trees, curled up in a nest of leaves. She felt safe enough there, assuming that the trees would protect her. By midafternoon she was off again, traveling as quickly as she could.

If she were a Meerimec, the trees might sing her home, or at least that was what Loba called her style of travel. She'd shown

Tanelith some of her magic just before she'd left, racing up the trunk of one of the great trees then leaping easily from branch to branch. She traveled as quickly through the canopy as Tanelith did across the ground.

Did all Meerimec have that ability? Tanelith wasn't sure, and she really didn't have anyone to ask. Hopefully nothing had happened to Loba and Tanelith would be able to ask her.

That sense of urgency took over her again, as persistent as the cold nipping at her cheeks.

Worried, Tanelith pressed forward, following the path the trees made for her. It still took her another day to reach the inner edge of the guardian trees, making her way into the normal woods, where there were many types of trees. Frost tipped the edges of the grass, and it had snowed here recently. Fortunately, the path the guardian trees had made for her ended right at the edge of a small creek that hadn't frozen over yet.

Tanelith followed along an animal track that the deer and others had beat down next to the creek. She was exhausted, but she was also certain that she needed to hurry.

Hopefully, she wouldn't arrive at Loba's house too late.

CHAPTER

THREE

Loba's house looked much the same as the first time Tanelith had seen it. At least this time she knew to look for it, and didn't nearly walk into it. It was midmorning, and she'd been traveling most of the night. The air was crisp and cool, with clouds overhead, promising more snow.

The house was perfectly round, built on stilts above the creek. The wooden walls still had bark on them, which made the house blend in to its surroundings. Reddish-green moss grew on the conical roof, giving it a fuzzy appearance. Round windows had been cut into the walls. They looked like dark eyes, peering in all directions. A porch ran all the way around the house, though there was nothing on it.

Tanelith knew that in many ways, what she saw was an illusion. There was a round house there, on stilts, with a conical roof and a porch. However, the house currently in front of her looked as though no one had lived there for years. There were no stairs going up to the porch, no doorway either.

It was how the house protected itself. Loba had said that any honest traveler with need would be able to find the entrance. However, anyone with ill-intent would never find their way in.

The creek ran from east to west. Tanelith walked to the

southern part of the house, to one of the larger posts that supported the porch. Loba had carved all of them. Some of the designs were representational, with birds, vines, and plants decorating them. Others were more abstract. Tanelith had always thought that the one closest to the door had a blowing pattern on it, like wind streaking through the clouds.

Tanelith reached up and knocked on the post. Loba had told Tanelith that she would always be welcome in her house. It worried her that the illusion had stayed up for so long, that it hadn't dissolved as she approached.

Now, though, it was as if a mist melted all around the house, revealing the true house. The walls remained the same, as did the porch and the roof. But stairs appeared, and smoke started puffing out of the center of the roof. Wind chimes tinkled softly hanging on either side of the open door. The windows retained their round shape, but now they appeared more lively and not like blank, hard eyes.

Was Loba not at home? Was that why the house had taken so long to recognize her? No, there was a fire going in the wood stove that sat in the center of the house. Someone was there.

Tanelith walked up the stairs warily. She didn't see anything out of order on the porch. Loba's rocking chair was still beside the door. A piece of wood sat on the small table next to it, the latest of Loba's whittling projects. She couldn't hear anyone talking inside, though she did smell the marvelous barley soup that Loba had on to cook.

"Hello?" Tanelith called as she cautiously stepped through the door. It was a little dim inside, so she paused for a moment, blinking and clearing her eyes.

Movement from behind the wood-burning stove. Someone approached her.

It wasn't Loba, though it was a Meerimec. He had dark curly hair and blue eyes. The top of his head might have reached Tanelith's collarbone. He was very muscular, and just wore a vest for a top. For trousers, he wore something similar to what Loba always wore, short dark pants that were cuffed just below the knee, with tall boots.

It took Tanelith a moment to recognize the vest that the person wore.

It was made from a light brown leather, with red and gold cloth edging the armholes as well as running down the front in wider plaques.

Slaves wore those vests.

In the blink of an eye, Tanelith pulled the Dissolving Blade out of her pack and had it pointed toward the person. It changed as she'd unsheathed it, transforming from its ceremonial appearance to a long, milky-white sword.

The handpiece she always wore transformed as well. Normally, it appeared as a heavy mesh triangle that had grown into the back of her hand. It was held in place by thick bands around her thumb, middle and pinky fingers, as well as a wide cuff around her wrist.

Now, it became a war gauntlet, made out of the milky-white glass armor that was impenetrable. Sharp spikes rose up along the outside of her arm.

While Tanelith could completely suit up in the same armor, she stopped when the slaver raised his hands, showing they were empty. "I'm not here to hurt Loba!" he said urgently.

"Why should I believe you?" Tanelith said. She gestured with the sword that he should move to the side so that she could approach the area of the room where Loba generally slept.

"'Cause he's my idiot of a grandson. Vyncis." Loba said. Her voice sounded terrible, scratchy and worn. "I called him here."

"He's a slaver," Tanelith said. She never looked away from Vyncis, never let her sword waver. If he moved suddenly in any direction, she'd skewer him.

She might not even regret it.

"I know," Loba said with a sigh. "Ye can call me a fool for not knowing."

"What do you mean?" Tanelith said. Looking at Vyncis, she

could see something of a family resemblance. He had the same round, high cheekbones as Loba, the same little pert nose. His eyes were a brighter blue, but that might be his youth.

"When ye first came, ye told me of the slavers. What they wore. Knew I'd seen the outfit. Hadn't realized what it meant," Loba said. "Now, put down that sword. Ye ain't killing him. Not yet. Not 'til he's done his penance."

Tanelith really, *really* didn't want to release the Dissolving Blade. She was being hunted by the slavers.

"How do I know that Vyncis won't slip off at the first chance and tell the others that he's seen me?" Tanelith said.

Loba gave a low chuckle. "He made his choice. Afore you came. It was either be a Meerimec, or a slaver. Ye can't be both, boy."

"Loba is telling the truth," Vyncis said. His accent was much smoother than his grandmother's. He'd spent a lot of time speaking the common tongue with the other races, that much Tanelith could tell. "I've given up being a slaver."

"For now? Or for always?" Tanelith asked.

Vyncis sighed, then nodded. "For always," he said.

Though the words were spoken softly, they carried a weight with them, as if a solemn bell had just tolled.

Tanelith knew that Loba valued the truth. The old woman claimed it was the secret behind her powerful illusion magic— that you could only disguise something if you knew the truth of it.

"I will hold you to your word," Tanelith vowed. She released the Dissolving Blade. It took a little effort to coax it back down into the form of a ceremonial dagger. It seemed to recognize that she was in potential danger and it wanted to protect her.

"Can I see that?" Vyncis asked.

Tanelith held the blade sideways so he could see the design of it. In its ceremonial form, the Dissolving Blade had bas relief designs all along the base of the blade, curling circles and lines. It made the blade as thick as her pinky finger was long. The metal was a cloudy gray, and the edge of the knife was dull, as though it had never been sharpened.

"And that became that sword?" Vyncis said, awed.

"It did," Tanelith said. "It's called a Dissolving Blade, and it will cut through anything. Even blood metal."

Vyncis blinked, then shook his head. Obviously, he didn't believe her.

Tanelith turned her head to the side so he could see the blood-red scar on the side of her neck. Then she showed him the other side. One of the scars was straight, the other was a wiggly line.

"I used the Dissolving Blade to cut the slave collar from around my neck," Tanelith said.

Vyncis' eyes grew wide. His mouth opened then shut again. "You escaped?" he asked, incredulous.

"I did."

Vyncis sagged at that. Finally, he said, "I understand."

Tanelith wondered if he actually did, if he knew just how hard the other slavers were coming after her.

Would he betray her? She had no idea.

"Now, if ye don't mind, this old woman needs some rest," Loba said, her voice cracking.

"I apologize," Tanelith said. "I will leave immediately," she added stiffly. She had needed Loba's help. She didn't want to go. But she didn't want to get any closer to this damned slaver than she had to. Plus, she had to get gone before he betrayed her.

"No," Loba said forcefully. "Ye will stay and keep me comfort these last days left to me."

Horrified, Tanelith finally hurried over to Loba.

The old woman appeared shrunken in on herself. Her skin had been the color of aged oak. Now, it had grayed, like driftwood. The wrinkles in her face looked deeper, as if they'd been etched with a charcoal pencil. Her blue eyes had faded further, making the irises difficult to distinguish from the whites.

She lay on a pile of furs, close to the wood stove. Just past her was a second pile. It seemed that Vyncis had been there for a while, taking care of his grandmother.

"What happened?" Tanelith asked. The last time she'd seen Loba, the Meerimec had appeared to be in good health.

Loba chuckled. "I'm old," she said. "It's my time." She sighed. "Would 'ave liked to see yer war. Won't make it to the new year, though."

Like the Egarlorsar, the Meerimec celebrated the new year after the longest night of the year, which was only a month away.

"Are you sure you want me to stay?" Tanelith said. It was a small, one room house. Three people would make it much more crowded.

"Why'd ye come to see me?" Loba shot back, some of the old fire returning.

Tanelith glanced over her shoulder at Vyncis. She was hesitant to talk about the city of the gods that she'd seen floating.

"I know ye don't trust 'im. I know ye got yer reasons. But yer gonna need the Meerimec if yer intent to bring the war to stop the slaving," Loba said. "He'll abide by his word."

"While you're alive," Tanelith pointed out.

Loba gave her a sly smile. "I got me ways to make sure he stays true. If he returns to the slavers, he'll never be able to come back to Gishem Woods. The guardian trees won't let him pass."

"I'd rather be a Meerimec than a slaver," Vyncis offered stepping closer, beside Tanelith. "I'd forgotten how good it felt here, in the woods. I...I didn't like what I did before."

"How could you have stood it at all?" Tanelith said. "To degrade people that way?" She tried not to get angry, but her tone was still harsh and bitter.

"Ye can talk of that later. Tell me why yer here," Loba insisted. "Humor an old woman afore her nap."

"If, maybe, there's a chance that one of the floating cities still exists, how would I get there?" Tanelith said. It wasn't the whole truth, but it was close enough. "How could I get up to the clouds?"

"Eh," Loba said, nodding and looking thoughtful. "I see. I know the people from the Broken Mountains have always believed they still fly. Do you, now?"

Tanelith wanted to lie. To merely shrug and say, "Maybe."

However, Loba would know it was a lie. For all she knew, Vyncis would as well.

"Yes," Tanelith said.

"Saw it, didn't you?" Loba pressed.

Tanelith paused. Did Loba think there were cities that still floated? Had she seen one, too?

"I did," Tanelith said.

Vyncis grew stiff beside her. Was he surprised? Shocked? Or had he known the truth as well?

The chuckle that Loba gave was unsettling. It sounded harsh and cackling.

"Oh, dearie, thank you," Loba said. "Ye have given me the key. I know where ye need to go. And I know how ye'll get there." She wheezed suddenly, coughing.

Vyncis rushed to the far side of his grandmother. He knelt, then helped her sit upright until the coughing fit was vanquished. She leaned on him heavily, as if she couldn't support herself.

Finally, when Loba could take a deep breath again, Vyncis laid her back down. "Sleep, grandmother," he said, kissing her tenderly on the forehead. "We'll both be here when you wake up."

Loba nodded tiredly and closed her eyes, appearing to fall asleep instantly.

Vyncis stood and gestured for Tanelith to follow him to the other end of the small room.

"There's soup, if you're hungry," he said. "Fresh bread, too." He looked at her critically. "Or do you need to rest? I can stay inside the house and you can sleep at the threshold, to make sure that I don't sneak off somewhere."

While Tanelith wanted to deny her exhaustion, she'd been pushing herself too hard for too long. The moon was also waning, not waxing, so her powers were weakening.

She helped herself to a small bowl of soup and some bread, then sat on a chair near the door, silently watching Vyncis.

He appeared to have picked up his grandmother's knack for carving, as he sat in a chair beside the wood stove in the center of the room, whittling.

Tanelith wondered at his skill, if it was something that all the Meerimec had. However, she didn't want to ask or talk with Vyncis, didn't want to engage with him, let alone trust him.

She was going to have to trust him a little, though, as the demands of the last few days made themselves known and she found her eyelids drooping.

After cleaning her dishes, Tanelith laid out her sleeping roll, right in front of the doorway, so that Vyncis couldn't get in or out without her knowing it. She slept with the Dissolving Blade in her hand, certain that it would awaken her if something was threatening her.

She didn't think that she'd sleep, but as soon as she closed her eyes she found herself drifting off, her dreams surprising warm and comforting, with Loba whispering in her ear of how great Tanelith's legend would be.

FOUR

It was dusk when Tanelith opened her eyes. The Dissolving Blade was still in her hand, her fingers curled loosely around the hilt.

She was in Loba's house. Vyncis didn't sit at the far end of the room. Loba did.

"Good, yer awake," Loba said. Her voice was still scratchy, though she looked better than when Tanelith had first seen her. Her skin was still gray, but she had more color in her cheeks. "Git yerself some dinner, then the three of us are gonna have a chat."

Vyncis was standing to the left, pulling up water from the creek that ran under the house. He said, "Yes, Grandmother," and went back to his chore.

Tanelith stood and stretched, keeping the blade in her hand, before she bent over and touched her toes. All her muscles felt stiff and slightly sore. She found herself automatically doing a few of the warrior poses that she'd been practicing with the sword, bending and stretching, as well as blocking and cutting.

It wasn't the full dance, she didn't really have time or space for that. It was enough, though, to get her loosened up. When she finished, she attached the blade to the belt on her waist.

While she'd been traveling, she'd left the dagger in her pack. It was too difficult to carry it in her hand all the time.

If it had just been Loba in the house, she would have left the blade with her pack. However, in the presence of Vyncis, she vowed to keep the sword with her at all times.

Vyncis had made what he called drop biscuits—large scoops of dough dropped into a dish then cooked in a clay pot over the stove. The dish was a spicy fish cooked with tomatoes and herbs. The drop biscuits turned out to be flaky and moist, delicious with everything else.

"Eat up, eat up!" Loba told both Vyncis and Tanelith. "Ye will need yer strength later," she promised them both with a sly twinkle in her eye.

When Tanelith looked at Vyncis, he gave a slight shrug. He had no idea what Loba was proposing either.

Tanelith told Loba of visiting the Broken Mountains, of how the people there were tall and proud, but living in the past. She also let Loba know that their Council of Elders had promised to welcome any of the slaves who Tanelith intended to free.

"Did you know that they turned away any of their children who didn't meet their ideal? Who were short, or who had curly hair?" Tanelith asked. It still made her angry enough to consider bringing war on her own people.

Loba shrugged. "I'd heard rumors, yes. But I couldn't believe it. Who would turn aside their own children? It couldn't be true."

"It is true," Tanelith said. "I wonder if that's how the slavers keep up their supplies, scooping up the rejected children, promising them a better life. Do you know?" Tanelith said, speaking directly to Vyncis for the first time that evening.

He bit his lips together and shook his head. "I didn't know. I didn't know where they got any of the slaves. But I also didn't work out here, either. I was in one of the Ilburh towns. Haedun."

"That's pretty far from here," Tanelith said. "I would have expected you to be in the closest town to Gishem Woods, in Faburh."

Vyncis sighed. "I think—I think the Gilukkhaz were afraid

that any of the Meerimec who were close to the woods would slip away, return there. So they sent us out to the other towns."

Faburh wasn't that close to Gishem Woods, it was still a good five to seven days away. Still, it made sense to separate Vyncis from his home and what he knew, if they wanted to turn him into a good slaver.

"Did you ever go on a slave raid? Capturing elves?" Tanelith asked. She had to know if he'd kidnapped people.

"No, I didn't," Vyncis said. "I couldn't handle the nets. Can't touch them without getting sick, or possibly dying."

"How could you be a slaver, then?" Tanelith said, confused. The Egarlorsar could wear the blood metal without dying. It just drained all their magic from them, until they learned how to control it.

She recalled that the Meerimec made lousy slaves because they couldn't be controlled. If they wore anything made from blood metal, they'd die after a few days, their blood clotted and no longer able to flow.

"I worked in an auction house," Vyncis said. "I never worked with any of the slaves directly."

"That's supposed to make it better?" Tanelith fumed.

"I needed the work," Vyncis said hotly. "It was that, or go begging in the market."

Tanelith had seen the beggars. They were broken people, as far as she could tell.

"You could have come back here," Tanelith said.

"And admitted that I was wrong?" Vyncis said. "That I couldn't travel as my grandmother had? That I didn't have what it took?"

"The world has changed," Loba interjected. "Traveling as I did—not sure it's possible, with the world as it is."

Vyncis shrugged. Tanelith could tell he was still bitter, that he felt as though he was a failure because he couldn't walk in his famous grandmother's footsteps.

She couldn't help him. Then she had to remind herself that she didn't *want* to help him, or to even like him.

"But ye still may be able to travel, at least to some places," Loba said. She nodded at Tanelith. "Said I knew of a place that might help ye. I do. It's called the Stairs of the Gods. Have ye heard of it?"

Tanelith thought for a moment. She vaguely recalled seeing such a place marked on the large map that Arryn had spread out on his dining room table.

Arryn—the Ilburh who'd bought her as a slave, who she'd killed as he was trying to rape her.

"Maybe," Tanelith said. "It's to the south, in the desert, right?"

"Aye," Loba said. "The desert is harsh in that area. Not much water. The landscape is truly amazing though. Red rocks, piled up on top of one another, reaching all the way to the sky. Tiny bunches of scrub clinging to the sides of the towers. The air always smelled like cinnamon and sage. I'd never been somewhere so open, where the stars cover the sky like a blanket of lights."

The old woman gave Tanelith a soft smile. "That's where ye need to go. While there are lots of rocks around, there's a formation called the Stairs. It's taller than the others, reaches right up and brushes the clouds. I heard stories of people going there, climbing up to the top, and disappearing, never to be seen again. Your people."

Tanelith blinked, surprised. That certainly sounded like it might be the right place—a staircase that led up to the sky.

"How do I get there?" Tanelith said. She could probably make it to the desert herself, though she'd be crossing Ilburh lands to get there. Once she was in the desert, she'd have to be careful. The burning sun would weaken her. Plus, at the western edge of the desert stood the Nyramukz mountain, the home of the Gilukkhaz. And underneath those mountains were slave mines.

When Tanelith had been kidnapped by the slaver Ugmas,

she'd been following a young couple. The slavers had sent all the females to the towns, while the males were all sent to the mines.

"If I was younger, I'd go with ye. In a heartbeat," Loba said, sounding sad. "Oh, I wish I could. To go see such sights again." She sighed, then she nodded at Vyncis. "He'll have to go in my place. Be your guide."

"What?" Vyncis said.

"No," Tanelith said at the same time. "He's never been there. How could he lead me there?"

"We'll do a heart share," Loba said.

Now, it was Vyncis' turn to say, "No."

Tanelith shook her head. "What is that?"

"I will share me memories with me grandson," Loba said. "He'll know where to find water, how to look for it in case the old oasis are gone dry. He'll also know exactly where the Stairs of the Gods are."

"It will kill you," Vyncis said coldly. "I don't want that hanging on my head."

"Boy, I'm dead all ready," Loba said. "It's gonna be part of yer penance. To lead Tanelith to the Stairs, and to make sure she's successful."

Tanelith didn't like the sounds of any of this. "You could draw a map, or just tell us stories about your travels there," she said.

"Ye won't succeed," Loba said firmly. "Plus, it's the best way for the youngster to atone for his misdeeds. I've made up my mind."

"What?" Vyncis said. "No, that's not possible."

"How have yer dreams been lately?" Loba asked, giving Vyncis a broad wink.

Vyncis shuddered. "That was you?" He took a deep breath. "That was you," he said again, this time flatly, no longer questioning.

"Aye," Loba said. "It weren't that ye lacked courage, dearie. Ye coulda made it. Ye didn't have the knowledge ye needed. Remember, I didn't start my travels until after my first babe."

"My mother, who you abandoned," Vyncis said.

Tanelith wondered at the lack of bitterness in his tone. Instead, it sounded like a story that had been repeated many, many times, all the emotion worn off through all the retellings.

"She was much better off with my sister than with me," Loba said, her chin coming up stubbornly. "I wouldn't a been a good mother to her. Or to ye."

Tanelith had wondered when Loba had had time to have and raise a child, particularly given how long and far she'd traveled.

It seemed to be an old argument between them. Vyncis stared hard at her but finally nodded.

"So what is this thing you want to do? A heart share?" Tanelith asked.

"I can share my memories with one other Meerimec. Can't really do anyone else. Sorry, dear, I did try," Loba said.

Tanelith nodded slowly. She remembered her dreams from the night before, feeling as though Loba was whispering to her the entire time she slept.

"Can only be someone close," Loba said. "Like a son or daughter."

"Or a grandson," Vyncis added. "Did ye ever think to ask if it was what I wanted?"

"No," Loba said, sounding stubborn again. "Ye don't get to choose yer penance."

Vyncis had the same look on his face as his grandmother, stubborn and angry.

"What if I don't want to lead her to these stairs? What if I refuse?" Vyncis said hotly.

"Then, me boy, ye'll leave these woods and never return," Loba said. "But ye better be going now, and get clear o' the trees, afore I die. And I'll be gone by morning."

"What?" Tanelith said.

"No!" Vyncis said. "Don't leave. Not yet."

"I've been holding on by a twig for days, now," Loba said. She nodded toward Tanelith. "Knew ye were coming, as soon as ye crossed into the woods. Wanted to see ye again. And that shiny sword o' yers."

Loba's voice was growing weaker, and her accent, rougher. The color she'd had in her cheeks when they'd started dinner had faded.

"I'm so sorry, I wish I'd known. I would have gotten here sooner, if I could," Tanelith said.

"Ye came when ye could," Loba said. Then she fixed a hard eye on her grandson. "So what's yer choice? Are ye a Meerimec? Or something else?"

"Not like it's a real choice, is it?" Vyncis said bitterly. "I'll agree to the heart share. To leading her to the stairs."

"Not just that—ye gotta promise ye'll make sure Tanelith's successful," Loba said.

"I'll do everything I can to make sure she succeeds," Vyncis said. "But there are slavers coming after her. If they capture her, there's not a lot I can do."

"Sure there is," Loba said. "Ye can rescue her. Or at least try yer best. The trees will know what's in yer heart."

Vyncis nodded, though he still looked stubborn. "I will do what I can."

Tanelith doubted that.

"That's all I ask," Loba said. She suddenly appeared to shrink in on herself. "Take me to me bed," she said, her voice barely above a whisper. "Ye lay down on yers. And dream."

Then she turned a hard gaze to Tanelith. "Ye take that shiny sword of yers, and make sure none disturb us. Not wind, not rain, not other folks. Ye stand guard over us, ye hear me?"

"I will protect you with my life," Tanelith promised, surprised to be included.

"Aye," Loba said. "Ye'll do fine. Goodbye, dearie. Happy travels. I enjoyed knowing ye."

"Goodbye," Tanelith said. The shock of her words choked her

throat. Was she really saying goodbye to this fascinating old person? She'd never met anyone like Loba. The world would be colder—and less interesting—with her gone.

Loba looked at Vyncis, who nodded and stood. He lifted Loba out of her chair as if she weighed nothing, then laid her down on her bedding. The old woman appeared to already be asleep.

Vyncis looked at Tanelith, his blue eyes drilling into her. "If anything disturbs us, either of us, we'll both die," he said harshly. "And while I know you might not care for me, I hope that you care enough for my grandmother to see that she gets her dying wish."

"I will guard both of you," Tanelith said. She unsheathed the dagger, and this time let the full transformation occur, until she was standing there facing the ex-slaver in a full suit of milky-white armor. Spiked gauntlets covered her hands and arms, sharp pointed boots her feet. Every part of her glowed, like moonlight through an open window. She left the helm open, so her face was still visible.

"Nothing shall get through me to disturb you," Tanelith promised.

Vyncis' eyes were wide with astonishment. "Grandmother had mentioned that you might bring a war with you, when you returned from the Broken Mountains. Now, I see why."

He nodded at her, then pushed the furs he'd been sleeping in closer to his grandmother. He laid down and took her hand. In a few moments, his face was slack with sleep.

Tanelith turned away from the sleepers. She didn't know who —or what—might try to disturb them.

They would have to kill her to reach them, though.

CHAPTER

FIVE

Night settled in outside of the house. Tanelith could see just fine in the dark, so she didn't bother lighting more candles. The half-dozen or so that were already lit created pools of light, with heavy shadows in between.

Tanelith wasn't sure what she was up against. Would someone actually try to come in the door? Wouldn't the house protect itself from someone with ill intent?

Maybe. But maybe the power of the house would be taken up with Loba's dying. Tanelith didn't know how much magic the house held in itself and how much came from the old Meerimec.

The sleepers held hands, each on their separate collection of furs. Neither of them had pulled anything over their bodies, so Tanelith added another log to the fire in the wood-burning stove, to keep the house warm.

Loba still looked shrunken in on herself. If she stood, the top of her head might not reach Tanelith's chest. The veins on her uncovered legs pushed out, the muscles there withering.

Would there be anything left but a husk by morning? Tanelith didn't want to be fascinated by the process—that was her friend there, dying—yet she didn't want to look away.

When nothing additional changed after a while, Tanelith did

shift her attention away from the sleepers to the rest of Loba's house.

On the back wall, opposite the door, a full-sized carving of a doe stood underneath shelves holding tiny statues, looking up, as if she were startled from her drinking from a creek. Hanging from the ceiling were more carvings. They weren't wind chimes, as the pieces would never touch. But more than one flock of birds flew on strings, hanging from sticks that were connected. A flock of colorful fish swam through the air. Another was made up of tiny trees, each one intricately carved and painted gold.

Other creatures populated the shelves: a cricket, a large moth, even a pair of small bear cubs, rolling over each other, playing. A small box sat beside them, about the length of Tanelith's palm, with leaves carved into it, holding unknown treasures.

A snake lay on one of the shelves. Had that been there the first time Tanelith had stayed with Loba? She didn't remember it from before. It seemed incomplete, as if it had been pressed out of wood, not carved. The scales were hinted at, not individually carved, unlike the tiny trees, which had each leaf detailed. Only the fangs looked realistic to her, sharp as needles.

Was that Vyncis' work? Not Loba's? There was a look to the snake's eyes that she didn't trust.

She reached out to touch it, nearly shrieking when it suddenly moved. Its wide gaping mouth snapped at her. She drew back fast enough that it didn't strike her.

A flush ran across the wood back of the snake. The scales grew distinct bands of black and red, separated by smaller rings of white. Beady eyes stared at her from its black face as it flicked its forked tongue.

It fixed its attention for a moment on the two sleepers behind Tanelith, before returning its gaze to her.

Some warning from the Dissolving Blade had Tanelith moving before the snake launched itself at her, aiming directly for her face.

She got her arm up in time to block the attack, so the snake's fangs didn't reach her skin but instead, closed on her gauntlet, hanging on.

Was that a look of surprise?

The snake had grown huge in the last few heartbeats. Originally, it had been as long as her forearm. Now, its tail hung past her knees.

With her other hand, Tanelith grabbed the snake right behind the jaws, so it couldn't turn its head and bite her again. The tail thrashed as she pulled it off her gauntlet. The fangs hadn't penetrated, but they would have bitten through anything other than her armor. She held the snake out away from her body so it wouldn't wrap around her, entangling her in its coils.

Now what? She couldn't kill it—it was far too difficult to get it to stay still long enough for her to swing her blade. And she wasn't strong enough, even with the gauntlet, to crush it.

Plus, somehow she knew that the death of such a creature might bother its creator, and she didn't want to disturb either Loba or Vyncis.

After looking around for a moment, Tanelith walked over to the hinged opening in the floor, that allowed Loba to pull buckets of water up to the kitchen from the creek below. She kicked open the hatch.

Instead of the friendly water burbling below, all she saw were rolling dark clouds.

She hesitated a moment, then dropped the snake into them. *From darkness, to darkness,* was the only thing she could think of at the time.

Then she quickly closed the hatch, making sure that it was latched, so that it wouldn't be easy for anything to crawl back into the house.

She glanced up at the windows. It was dark outside the house. Much darker than it should be. It was if a black fog was pressed in on all sides.

Loba's house didn't have a proper door, nothing to shut the inside off from the outside. Normally, Tanelith could see trees out the door, just past the posts holding up the porch. She would hear the creek trickling past. The familiar smells of grass and pines would swirl up to greet her.

Now, nothing stood outside the house except empty darkness. Mists and shadows wrapped around, blocking all sight and sound. Even the smell of the woods had faded.

Was this Loba's magic? To keep anything from disturbing her during the heart sharing? Maybe this was the house, looking to protect its maker? Or was it something else, something much darker, biding its time until it could enter?

Tanelith whispered a quiet prayer to the Hidden One, the god who crept through the shadows, the Nameless and Faceless one who had saved her people when the cities had fallen. She asked the Hidden One to keep them all safe, to help her ride out the night.

Then she walked back over to where the sleepers lay. They both looked worn, the process draining them.

She wished again that there was something more she could have done to save Loba, though she knew that even the gods couldn't turn back time.

Still, she asked that her Goddess Celionael look over the pair of them.

A loud *crack* answered her prayer.

Startled, Tanelith widened her stance, to what she always thought of as her warrior position.

A shiver went through the entire house, the floor bouncing slightly, as if a great tree had just fallen in the woods.

When Tanelith turned away from the sleepers, she saw a dark column forming just past the shelves with the carved wooden figures. Its appeared to have risen from underneath the house, bursting through the floor and now pushing against the ceiling. It was about the width of a fat man and carried the stench of rotting soil. A chill raced across her back.

As Tanelith watched, the blackness coalesced. The main body of the column became a tree trunk with rough black bark. Odd bulges grew out of its sides. It seeped red sap that she instinctively knew was poisonous.

Quickly, a proliferation of branches formed at the top of the tree. They spread across the ceiling.

Just as quickly, Tanelith used her blade to cut off the branches that were heading in the direction of the sleepers.

More branches grew, though this time they weren't focused up, but out. They bristled with thorns and dripped with poisonous sap. They reached out to smack her or entangle her.

Tanelith had never imagined that the first opponent she'd fight would be a tree. She lopped off branches, then ran the blade along the edge of a branch to shore off all the thorns. She deflected twigs and leaves shot in her direction. At least there were no roots crossing the floor, entangling her feet.

It was tiring work. Tanelith knew that the moon was waning, so her magical strength wasn't at its height. The tree appeared to be able to endlessly regenerate branches.

Just defending herself and keeping the tree branches from the sleepers wasn't going to be enough. She was going to have to defeat it, and soon, before her strength ran out. She couldn't rely on the sword. It only knew how to defend or attack. It couldn't plan a way out of an encounter.

At the next opening, Tanelith tried to get closer in, to stab at the trunk of the tree. A limb came crashing down on her helmet for her effort. She stepped back quickly, slightly dazed.

Still, she knew that was what she needed to do.

Tanelith stayed in close, pushing in closer every chance she got. The arm holding the sword was a blur as she cut off limb after limb. She blocked attacks with her other hand, punching branches that shot out at her like an angry dwarf in a bar fight.

Finally, step after slow step, she was close enough to strike the torso of the tree.

The first cut wasn't fatal, for all that it made the trunk bleed red sap.

However, the tree did slow down now. It wasn't throwing as

many branches at her. Tanelith was able to keep her position, close into the trunk, slashing and hacking at the main torso of the monster she fought.

Tanelith realized that the tree was about to fall over. She reached back with her arms and sank her sword deep into the heart of the beast.

Again, the house shivered, a cold wind blowing through the wide room.

When Tanelith pulled her sword from the trunk of the tree, it started shrinking in on itself. The bark grew less distinct again, until all that was left was the single column of black smoke.

Tanelith put both hands on the hilt of her sword and swung it low, like a farmer swinging a scythe. She chopped through the remaining smoke.

It disintegrated with a sifting noise, like ashes falling from a hearth.

Tanelith stood there panting for a moment, trying to catch her breath.

What had that thing been? The branches she'd cut off were even now withering and dissolving into nothingness. In a few more heartbeats, nothing remained of her great battle except her exhaustion and sore muscles.

Tanelith paused and took a deep drink of water from the jug Loba had on the counter. She was about to go take a look at the sleepers when a noise made her freeze.

The sound of chains.

Slavers.

While fighting the massive black tree, Tanelith had known fear, but she hadn't been too afraid. She hadn't necessarily known what she was doing. She still had belief that she could defeat the monster in front of her.

Slavers though. Here. In Gishem Woods. How could she stop them? Should she run out of the house so they'd follow her? Leave the sleepers be?

She turned slowly, then froze. Her worst nightmare stood before her eyes, just inside the door.

Ugmas the slaver looked just as ugly as she remembered him being. What little hair he had on his head stuck out on all sides, like a dark mane. His large, round eyes glared with hate at her. Finger bones and nuggets of blood metal had been braided into the full beard that went down to the middle of his chest. He proudly wore a leather vest, decorated around the arms and edges with gold and red. Bowed legs stuck of short pants. Muscles stood up across his torso and bare arms.

He had a net in his hands. Tanelith remembered those nets. She still had nightmares of being entangled in them. They had wires of blood metal woven into them. Touching one with her bare hands would leave her powerless. She'd been successfully able to cut one with her sword, though, when she'd fought off the slavers before.

Tanelith swallowed against a dry throat, watching Ugmas slowly stalk toward the sleepers. She tried to get herself to move but found herself frozen. She had to stop him! Now!

But...how had he gotten here? Why hadn't the guardian trees stopped him?

She tried to bring her sword up. If weighed three times what it normally did. Was that her fear? Or was it reacting to the blood metal in the room?

Except...her sword hadn't been bothered by the blood metal before. Plus, she just noticed that the glow of her armor had diminished. She didn't believe that her fight with the evil tree had drained her that much.

No, her sword and her armor should be lit up like the full moon in the presence of her enemy.

Which meant this wasn't real. It was an illusion. A dream.

"You are not here," Tanelith said quietly, her words just above a whisper. She lowered her sword.

If she was wrong, she'd just ended all of their lives.

"You are merely an illusion."

Still, Ugmas walked forward. Just two more steps and he'd throw his net on the sleepers.

"You are just my own fears, manifest."

With that, Tanelith forced herself to close her eyes.

She kept herself tense, ready to defend herself, to leap into battle.

Nothing happened for several long, tense moments.

The sound of the chains disappeared.

When Tanelith opened her eyes, Ugmas had vanished and dawn was peeking through the windows.

Trees stood outside again. The creek burbled its greeting to her. Birds chirped and flitted from branch to branch. A cool wind caressed her cheek, carrying the promise of more snow.

A soft, startled cry made Tanelith rush over to where the sleepers lay.

Loba was dead. Tanelith knew that just from looking at her. Her skin was completely gray now, like wood that had been dried too long in the sun. Death seemed to have taken the old Meerimec by surprise, her completely pale eyes wide open and unseeing.

Vyncis sat up from where he'd been laying. He shook his head, looking around, obviously seeing the world with new eyes. Then he tenderly reached over and shut his grandmother's eyes.

"She's gone," he said. Possibly it was just something he'd needed to say.

Tanelith's sorrow weighed heavily on her, along with her exhaustion. Though she might have only been fighting dreams all night, she still felt as though it had been one long battle. She transformed the Dissolving Blade, withdrawing her armor.

"Now, we wait for the others, for the funeral and the burial," Vyncis said. His gaze was curious, and Tanelith knew that she'd have a lot of questions to answer later.

"Others?" Tanelith asked, delaying the inquisition for a bit.

"Family," Vyncis said. "My mother. Loba's other sister. Some friends who Loba thought were important enough to tell of her coming death."

Tanelith nodded, though she wasn't sure how Loba had managed that. Had her spirit gone to visit them during the long night?

She paused, then decided she needed to ask anyway. "Was the sharing successful?"

Vyncis drew his legs up and rested his head against his knees. "It was," he said softly. "I can guide you where you need to go. It will take a few days for me to figure out everything. The sharing wasn't...wasn't in order." He gave her a sweet smile. "Loba's stories came as one thing related to another. It wasn't told to me as she'd experienced it, but as she remembered it, in pieces and bits and bobs."

"All right," Tanelith said. "You should rest," she added, holding back her own questions. She knew that while Vyncis had been sleeping all night, he hadn't actually been resting, but in a dream state with his grandmother. "I'll keep watch."

"I suspect you'll be doing that a lot, while we're traveling," he said as he laid back down.

"Yes, I suspect I will," Tanelith said as she went over to the door, waiting for the others, impatient to get going, to find the destiny she was sure awaited for her.

It was much better to focus out, on her future, then on the heaviness of her heart or her sadness at her friend's passing.

SIX

The first to arrive later that morning was an older Meerimec woman, leading a group of three younger people, two males and one female. Tanelith recognized the family resemblance with Loba, the high round cheeks and small sharp nose.

"Hello," Tanelith said, greeting them from the porch.

The old woman looked Tanelith up and down, then gave a dismissive sniff. "Of course, knowing me sister, she would have *others* present," she said in a disgruntled voice as she made her way up the stairs. "I'm Mira, Loba's oldest sister."

As Tanelith stood, Mira continued. "Oh, yer a tall one, aintcha? Well, we'll have none of ye and yer proudful ways. I'm in charge now, and ye'll do what I say. Or leave."

She stood there with her arms crossed over her chest, obviously uninclined to shake hands or clasp forearms.

Tanelith remembered so many of the Ilburh who wouldn't look at her, or shake hands, who considered her an animal or worse. She trembled deep inside with rage, but she wouldn't allow this Meerimec to make her react. She kept her face blandly neutral, a trick she'd learned when she'd been a slave. Before she could say anything, she heard movement behind her.

"Hello, Aunt Mira," Vyncis said from the open doorway, his

voice even. "And since I'm here, and not only witnessed but shared the death, I am in charge. I know Loba's dying wish, and *you* will do as *I* say."

Fury twisted Mira's lips, but she pressed them tightly together and didn't say anything for a few moments. "Fine," she finally spat out. "We'll camp out here."

Without another word, she turned and marched down the steps, back out under the trees. While the two boys followed her quickly, the girl turned, smiled and waved at Vyncis, then scurried off after the others.

"My cousin Aldira is all right. She knows that there are worthwhile towns beyond Derwick, where we grew up, and that people who are not Meerimec matter," Vyncis said softly.

"What did Mira mean, that she was now in charge?" Tanelith said.

Vyncis sighed. "If a Meerimec dies alone, the first person who comes across the body can dispose of all property as they see fit. Whether or not it is in accord with the dead person's wishes. Aunt Mira would burn this house down to the ground, destroy all of Loba's carvings, perhaps even go so far as to bury her sister under the creek so no plant could grow up around her."

"Bad blood, I take it?" Tanelith said. The Egarlorsar didn't have contracts per se, but they did usually have more than one witness if there important matters to be dealt with after they'd died.

The Ilburh had it all in writing, a *will* they called it. Tanelith had never heard of such a thing before becoming a slave.

"Going way back," Vyncis said. "My mother didn't know her father. However, she always maintained that Great Aunt Mira knew. Possibly had even had her eye on the young man herself."

Tanelith nodded. That would have created some bad blood between the sisters.

"But Loba never married?" Tanelith said.

Vyncis shrugged. "Lots of people have babies and then later decide to get married. No shame in it, either way. The Gilukkhaz don't think it's a bad thing either. However, the Ilburh don't do it that way. They think that having a baby and not being married to be an awful thing."

Tanelith nodded. "The Egarlorsar prefer that the young people be married first. However, there's a saying about while it might take nine months for a regular birth, an eager bride might only taking six, as they've been extra blessed by the Goddess."

That made Vyncis smile. He still looked tired, but she could tell his strength was returning.

His attention turned from her and his eyes took on a distant look, searching through the woods. "My mother will be here soon, along with my other great aunt, Loba's younger sister. We need to start cooking if we're going to feed them all."

"What can I do to help?" Tanelith asked. Had Vyncis always had that ability? To sense people coming? Or had he gained it along with the memories from Loba?

It would have made him a powerful hunter, if he'd ever gone on a slave hunt.

"Could you catch some more fish?" Vyncis suggested. "We'll smoke some, make soup with the rest. Tonight, we'll feast outside the house. Tomorrow, we travel to bury Loba."

Tanelith remembered Loba telling her some of the death rites of the Meerimec, how the body was buried under their favorite tree or plant. It was a way of ensuring that all vegetation was honored, because you never knew when a bush or a tree might be inhabited by the soul of one of their own.

"Where are we going?" Tanelith asked, though she had a sneaking suspicion what the old Meerimec had considered her favorite plant.

"To the guardian trees," Vyncis said. "I know you can't travel as quickly through the woods as we can. I will carry you with us, so that we can get there in only a day."

Tanelith nodded. "Will we stay there over night?"

"Aye," Vyncis said. "Then, you and I, go on from there. To the desert and beyond."

A cold shiver went down Tanelith's spine at those words. Vyncis' eyes had grown dark, his gaze distant. He was no longer seeing her, but the days ahead.

Was he regretting his bargain with his grandmother? Did he fear the guardian trees? Or was it something else that made him look so worried?

"It will be fine," Tanelith said after a few moments.

Vyncis shook his head and smiled at her. "I'm sure it will be," he said, before he turned and went back inside the house.

Tanelith stood there for a moment shaking her head.

She was certain that Vyncis had just lied to her.

What did he know that she didn't?

SEVEN

The next Meerimec to approach the house didn't have a strong family resemblance to Loba. Her face was flatter and her eyes were green, not blue or gray.

At least she smiled at Tanelith as she came up. "Oh, so you must be the foreigner that Mira was ranting about. I'm Lirelli, Loba's daughter."

"Nice to meet you," Tanelith said. Her hands were purposefully full of a bucket and fishing gear, so that she didn't have to feel snubbed when the next person didn't want to shake her hand.

Lirelli gave her a warm smile. "Oh, don't let Mira bother you. She was certain that Loba had gold or silver hidden here someplace, that she wanted to inherit. I told her that my mother didn't treasure things, but experiences. Mira never listened."

Tanelith felt herself relax. While Lirelli didn't look much like her mother, she did have a similar warmth. "Sounds like you knew Loba well."

Lirelli shrugged. "We fought for years. I didn't know her at all. Not until I had my own children, who were each as different as roses are from turnips. Only then did I finally start understanding why my mother had chosen the life she had. We made up, though only recently. I don't think we were ever friends, but we were no longer enemies."

"Vyncis was here during Loba's death," Tanelith said. "They... shared." She didn't want to say more than that, but she felt as though Lirelli had a right to know.

"Did they?" Lirelli asked, raising one eyebrow. Then she sighed and shook her head. "I'd hoped, that since Vyncis had returned, that he might come home. I was always afraid that Loba's spirit inhabited him. Her stories of her travels lit a fire within him when he was a boy. I'd had hopes...But he's going to continue on, with you. Right?"

"Yes," Tanelith said. She didn't understand why she was bracing herself for a barrage. Lirelli seemed perfectly reasonable. She still found her back stiffening, her feet widening into the warrior pose, and she rested her forearm against the pommel of the dagger she had attached to her belt, as neither hand was free and she couldn't easily grab it.

Lirelli folded her arms over her chest and looked back toward the woods. Though her face was calm, Tanelith could tell that a tsunami of emotion raced through her core.

Finally, Lirelli turned back to face Tanelith. "Can you promise me that you'll take care of my boy?" she demanded.

"I will," Tanelith said solemnly. As long as he didn't revert to his slaver ways, she would protect her guide.

Lirelli peered at her for a few more moments, as if trying to seek out the armor around her soul. "The Meerimec have the gift of foretelling. Often, it isn't much. Just a feeling that you should stay home that morning, and an important visitor arrives, one who you would have missed. Or you go fishing at a different part of the river and have the greatest catch of your life. Little things that smooth out a life."

She shook her head. "I don't have a good feeling about you. There is a storm coming, and you are its herald."

Tanelith paused for a moment before she finally said slowly,

"Your mother wasn't sure if I would bring the war to end the slavery of my people, or if it would be my daughters."

Lirelli stilled at that. Her eyes took on a faraway look. "Oh, my," she said softly.

What was she seeing? Could she see the path ahead?

"You bring danger to my boy," Lirelli accused Tanelith coldly. "Just see that you bring him back here. His body if not his soul."

With that, she turned and left, leaving Tanelith standing shocked and surprised.

What kind of danger could Lirelli see? What were Vyncis and Tanelith walking into?

"I see you've met my mother," said Vyncis dryly from behind her.

"Yes," Tanelith said, turning to look at him.

He stood at the doorway of the house. He'd rolled up the sleeves of his brown shirt, and his hands were wet from being recently rinsed off. His brown curls looked neater than the last time Tanelith had seen him. Dark circles under his eyes still showed his exhaustion.

Vyncis shook his head. "She tried to wrap me in cotton batting when I was growing up. She always saw the worst of what could happen. Never the best. She's seen me dead in a ditch at least a hundred times." He sighed. "Loba was the one who encouraged me to explore, to pick myself back up again when something went wrong. I didn't see my grandmother often—she was always away traveling. But when she did come back, she'd be here for a year. Then she'd be off again."

"That must have been difficult," Tanelith said. She'd had her own issues while growing up, having to take care of her twin sisters.

She still missed them terribly.

Vyncis shrugged. "It's family," he said. He looked off for a few moments. "You go get some more fish. I'll greet the next guests. We'll get a couple more people today, but the last won't arrive until after dark."

"What do you see?" Tanelith had to ask. "When you look into the future, traveling with me?"

Vyncis looked at her strangely. "I don't see anything at all," he said coldly. "I don't see us dying. I also don't see us living. The future for us is too unsettled. It's too important. Only heroes can see the important events. Like Heobo."

"Or Loba," Tanelith reminded him.

"Why would you think that she was a hero?" was Vyncis' reply, before he disappeared back inside the house.

Tanelith stood where she was for a few moments, wondering.

Would Loba be considered a hero to her people? She'd done many things that the others merely dreamed about. Traveled all across Ithlond, from the endless oceans to the west to the impenetrable forests of the east. Down to the dessert and up to the Wastelands.

She'd been strong magically as well, at least as far as Tanelith could tell. Loba wasn't as great a hero as Heobo had been, not according to the tales that Loba had told Tanelith.

Maybe she would be honored as a great hero by her people, though.

Tanelith only had to wait to find out.

In the meanwhile, there were fish to catch and a meal to prepare.

Plus, more secrets to learn.

EIGHT

Various cousins, Loba's other sister, and even a couple of friends arrived before nightfall. Tanelith helped Vyncis set up a number of places to sit outside the house: stumps, large boulders, buckets turned upside down. There was no long table they could serve food on, so they planned on using the edge of the porch to hold the dishes, and let people serve themselves.

No one was allowed to go inside the house yet. Tanelith wasn't exactly certain why—something to do with hospitality. Vyncis explained that after everyone had arrived, and they'd all eaten, there would be a viewing of the body.

"You will be expected to stand in line with everyone else," Vyncis said. "You'll probably be last in line, because you're not related or family."

"Or a Meerimec," Tanelith said wryly.

"That too," Vyncis admitted. He paused for a moment, thinking. "Unless you want to stand guard over the body? In your armor?"

"Would that be appropriate?" Tanelith asked.

Vyncis gave her a grin. "It sure would help with her legend. She's asked to be buried under the guardian trees. No one is buried there. No one but Heobo. I know that some in my family think that Loba's request is her being too full of herself. But I think she should be remembered as a great hero."

"Then I will stand behind the body, guarding it, in my full armor," Tanelith assured him.

"You can't fight anyone," Vyncis said seriously. "No matter what they say."

"As long as they don't touch the body," Tanelith said.

"Agreed," Vyncis said. "Though if someone wants one of her carvings, they may have it. Now, help me move this last log."

Tanelith was a little surprised at how informal the gathering felt as people started to come out from the trees. Vyncis didn't ring a bell or anything. Everyone appeared to just know that it was time.

While Tanelith had often found herself hunched over while she'd been in the Ilburh town, here, there was no point. The Meerimec were even shorter than the Ilburh. Most of them barely came up to her chest. The younger ones, though they were teenagers, were only half her height.

It was nice to share a meal with a family, even though it wasn't her family. Vyncis' cousin Aldira wanted to talk with Tanelith about where she was from. Like the others, she was curious about the elves. That Tanelith had come from the Broken Plains was treated with astonishment.

That Tanelith had been kidnapped by the Gilukkhaz and sold into slavery was less so.

The Meerimec knew that there were bad things happening out in the world. Heobo had told them that a second war was coming. They stayed in the trees, out of the light, hidden away.

It was as if they were also children of the Hidden One, and took the teachings of that god to heart.

Were all their houses like Loba's? She'd built hers, or encouraged the trees around it to shelter it, so that neither direct sunlight or moonlight struck it. Tanelith hadn't even seen the house that first time, not until she was practically on top of it. If she hadn't been following the creek, but had been on one of the game trails, she might have missed it entirely.

While her people had been ground down by the war, it felt to her as if the Meerimec were still afraid. Of what, she wasn't certain.

The last to arrive came as lovely rolls drizzled with a delightful sweet glaze were being served along with a strong herbal tea that tasted of mint and dark roasted roots. He stood at the edge of the clearing around Loba's house for a few moments, studying the crowd, before he walked forward.

Tanelith hadn't known he'd arrived. But Vyncis had. She'd been standing beside him when he suddenly stiffened.

"Hello, Son," came the words across the opening.

Vyncis turned, a false smile plastered across his face. "Hello, Father," he said.

Tanelith was confused. Hadn't she already been introduced to Vyncis' father? She threw a questioning glance at Vyncis, who replied softly, "My sire."

It suddenly all became clear. This was the man who'd fathered Vyncis, but not the one who'd raised him.

Lirelli sprang to her feet and walked over to confront the man. "What are you doing here?" she demanded, her arms crossed over her chest.

"I came to pay my respects," he said. His voice was soft but the words carried.

The Meerimec was older, much older than Tanelith would have expected. He looked more like Loba's peer rather than Lirelli's. His hair was all white and wrinkles were carved into his face. Even in the dim light his skin seemed golden, like beautiful aged maple. His shirt and pants were more finely made than any of the others, done in soft browns and tans, and a black cape hung over his shoulders.

Tanelith didn't see much of this beautiful figure in Vyncis, except perhaps their full lips and playful smile.

"You didn't even know my mother," Lirelli scoffed.

"I knew her better than you realize," the Meerimec said. "I sat at her hearth more than once, listening to her tell her tales as she whittled." He nodded toward the front porch. "I was often on the other rocking chair, singing to her. Is that so hard to believe?"

"No," Lirelli spat. "You loved her all along, didn't you? More than me."

"It isn't in my nature to settle down," he said. "Any more than it was your mother's."

Lirelli pressed her lips together as if she'd like to say something, anything, to get this man to leave.

However, he had every right to be there, just as she did, so Lirelli finally turned and walked away.

The man nodded at her retreating back, as if saying, "Thank you." Then he turned and walked over to Vyncis.

"Hello," he said, not offering to shake hands with his son.

Vyncis didn't look as though he would have taken his sire's hand anyway.

"And you must be Tanelith. I am Adas," he added with a sweeping bow, flicking back his cape dramatically.

"How do you know my name?" Tanelith asked, surprised. None of the others had even known she was here, not until Mira had ranted about it to them.

He gave her a charming smile. "Loba said you would do great things, and that I should seek you out one day, before I died. I am a poet. It is my hope that my words will live on, far past the death of the body."

Tanelith nodded. She knew of such bards among her people. They generally attended important events, like the meetings of the Council of Elders. Or maybe he wasn't here in an official capacity, but just as a friend.

"It is nice to meet you," Tanelith said. She was pleased that she and Vyncis had already decided that she would attend to the body in her full armor. Maybe Adas would help make Loba a legend.

As Adas was the last to arrive, he was quickly fed so that the funeral procession could begin.

Vyncis stood on the steps of the house with everyone assembled below. Tanelith stood beside him, facing the crowd. He'd insisted that she be there, though she'd heard more than one grumble from the assembled group that she was being too proud, that it wasn't her place.

"Friends, family, thank you for coming, for seeing to the burial of one of our greatest," he said.

Tanelith watched as some, like Mira, rolled her eyes at that pronouncement, while others, like Adas, merely nodded, as if expected.

"My grandmother Loba was unique in her generation," Vyncis said. "She traveled like Heobo, and was well-known amongst all the other races."

Tanelith knew that Vyncis was stretching the truth with that statement. While it was true that Loba had traveled, she wasn't well-known.

"Tonight, you will share your last words with her. Tomorrow, we will bury her according to her wishes, among the edges of the woods, under the guardian trees," Vyncis said.

"And if they won't take her?" Mira called out.

Tanelith was shocked. Why would they reject her? However, if the trees were truly aware, Mira might have a point.

Vyncis merely shrugged. "We will bury her near them, then," he said firmly.

"How will *she* get there?" Lirella asked, indicating Tanelith. At least she sounded polite enough with her question.

"I will take her with us," Vyncis said. "It is important that she, too, witness the burial."

Tanelith tried to stay solemn and peacefully look out at the dozen people gathered, instead of giving in to the shudder she felt.

The Egarlorsar didn't bury their dead. In fact, that was one of the curses they said to someone when they were angry: that their body should be buried on a moonless night.

Instead, the elves sat with the body and held an outdoor vigil, hopefully with the moon showing her brilliant face. At some point, the spirit would leave the body, and it would collapse in on itself. One moment, the shroud wrapped around the body would be full, the next, it would collapse in on itself, now holding merely a husk.

Tanelith had sat vigil with one of her grandmothers and seen it happen.

"Why her?" someone asked. She thought it was another one of Vyncis' cousins.

Vyncis took a moment to turn to look at Tanelith. Then he nodded at her and stepped to the side.

Tanelith pulled the dagger from her belt and slowly began the transformation. There was no direct moonlight, and the dark of the moon would be there the next night. However, she still pulled down what light she could into the gray dagger she held.

It changed color as it elongated, growing into the milky-white sword that she was familiar with.

People in the crowd gasped.

They cried out in astonishment as Tanelith continued the process. First the handpiece she always wore turned into a war gauntlet, covering her hand and forearm in milk-white glass armor. Spike grew along the side, sharp enough to slice flesh, strong enough to ram into brick. The armor continued to accumulate, spreading across her chest, down her other arm, then it covered her torso and finally her legs.

She left the face plate of the peaked helmet she wore open, so that those gathered could still see her. But she could completely engulf herself in armor should need arise.

As it had in the past, she knew it would again in the future.

"Tanelith stands before you as a warrior of the Egarlorsar, one of the guards of the Goddess Celionael," Vyncis said.

More gasps.

"She will guard the body as you view it," he added with another nod to Tanelith, who turned and went into the house, walking over to where Loba still lay on her furs.

Vyncis had put flowers all around the body. Possibly it was to hide the smell of decay that Loba's body was already exuding. It wasn't a bad smell, but rather, the smell of compost as leaves and twigs broke down to become soil.

Loba looked pitifully small laying there. She stood so much larger in Tanelith's memory.

Before Tanelith could say anything, Mira came in. As she was eldest, that was her right.

She marched right over to where Tanelith was standing. After a single glace at Tanelith, Mira focused on the body.

Tanelith could tell that Mira was angry about everything: Loba dying without revealing her treasures, that Loba had both Tanelith and Adas here, that Vyncis was her heir.

She didn't kick the body or spit on it, though Tanelith wouldn't have been surprised by either action.

After a disapproving sniff, Mira walked past. She threw a disdainful look at the shelves with all the carvings on them, then walked out with her head held high.

Loba's other sister came next. Tanelith couldn't remember her name. She looked sadly at her sister's body, wishing her a safe journey before she left.

One by one, the others came in to pay their respects. Most took a carving with them. Aldira took one of the hanging pieces, with all the birds on them. "She taught me how to call the birds, and sing with them," she admitted shyly before she left.

Adas came in somewhere in the middle of the line of viewers. He paused as he looked at Loba, then said, "I'm sorry that I won't be able to hear about any more of your travels. Though, if I know you, you're probably off having the grandest adventure of your life right now."

Then he speared Tanelith with a look. "As for you, I want your promise that you'll come and tell me all about your adventures when the time is right."

"I will," Tanelith said softly. Though she didn't know Adas, he struck her as elegant as any of Egarlorsar. He would have fit in at the Council of Elders in the Broken Mountains. They would have loved to hear his stories, hanging on every word of that honeyed tone.

Vyncis was last. He looked beyond exhausted, his skin gray and all the light leached from his blue eyes. "Ah, grandmother. Such a task you've given me. Not only to ensure that your legend remains, but that mine should be built on it." He shook his head, then softly said, "Good night, Grandmother."

He didn't take a carving from the shelf. Instead, he took Loba's whittling knife.

That left just Tanelith. She bowed her head and whispered, "Take care, Loba. Thank you for all the hospitality you've shown me. I'll make sure Vyncis is all right, that he stays on his path and pays his penance."

She paused, then she added the usual benediction of her people.

> *May you stay in the light of the Goddess, may the Moon guide your path, and may the Hidden One keep you safe.*

With that, she dismissed her armor and walked back out of the house. She didn't take any of the carvings. If she could have, she would have taken the deer, but she had no way to carry it, no place to store it.

Maybe some year she could get Vyncis to carve her something similar.

If they both survived.

CHAPTER

NINE

Though Tanelith went to sleep before most of the rest of the funeral party, morning still came far too early. She was a Moon Person and used to staying up all night. That part didn't bother her.

It was the getting up early that truly annoyed her.

But she woke when Vyncis did, packing up all of her belongings, as well as some extra food they'd carry with them. Then they served cold remains from the dinner the night before, along with plenty of hot tea as people started gathering around the house.

Vyncis had carefully wrapped Loba's body in a shroud the night before. She'd stayed out on the porch while they had slept inside.

"It used to be that our funerals were outside," Adas said, coming over to talk to Tanelith as people arrived and helped themselves to food.

"Our vigil, when the Egarlorsar sit with the body, still is," Tanelith said.

"Yes, I knew that. For us, the rites changed. It used to be that a body should feel both sunlight and moonlight before tasting the earth," he said. "Now, we are more hidden. Neither the sun or the moon touch us."

"Why is that?" Tanelith asked, curious.

Adas shrugged. "It started with The Uprising," he said.

At Tanelith's blank look, he added, "The War of Betrayal."

"Right," Tanelith said. She knew that other races had different names for the war when the great cities were destroyed. "The Ilburh call it The War of Freedom," she added, trying not to sound as bitter as she felt.

"And the Gilukkhaz call it The Great Reckoning," Adas said. "Four very different views of the same events." He paused, then added, "Heobo always predicted a second war, greater than the first. He claimed that it would tear families asunder. Some have mistakenly believed that if we stayed apart, stayed hidden, the next large conflict would pass us by."

"I think everyone hopes for that," Tanelith said. "No one really wants to go to war."

"I agree. But you've shown us that it is coming, that second war. And we will all be involved, whether we wish it or not. Not all are going to die as peacefully as Loba did," Adas said.

"I don't know," Tanelith said. "Loba said that it would either be me or my daughters who would bring the war to free my people."

Adas nodded. "I think it will be you." Then he gave her a broad smile. "Or at least, I hope it will be. I want to hear the accounts of your battles first hand, to start crafting the great epics that will be told about it afterward."

"You will not come and fight with us?" Tanelith teased.

Adas looked thoughtful at that. "A Meerimec warrior is astonishing to behold," he said seriously. "If you can see them. Just as your people play with shadows, so we trick the mind into seeing things that aren't really there."

Tanelith nodded. "Like Loba's house," she said.

"Yes, exactly," Adas said. "Loba was stronger than most. But I know a few young people who could have matched her. Who might be interested in stepping out of the woods and into the light."

Tanelith felt as though he was saying much more than just his spoken words. "I take it that you'll be talking with some of these young people, then?" she said casually. "Telling them what you saw here?"

"I'm in regular contact with them," Adas said seriously. "If you ever decide you need them, or need to call on the Meerimec, pass a message along to me."

"And how would I do that?" Tanelith asked. She felt as though fate was taking her by the hand and leading her, handing her some sort of Meerimec army when the time was right.

Adas gave her a pleasant smile. "Vyncis would know how," he said. He peered at her for a moment, before nodding once, as if he'd come to a decision. "Loba always sent one of her carved birds to me."

Tanelith's eyes widened. "I thought I'd dreamed that," she said.

Adas grinned at her. "I'm sure Loba meant for you to feel that way. But it was likely true."

"That was how she got Vyncis to come see her right away, wasn't it?" Tanelith said.

"And how she notified us all that she was dying," Adas said. "Although I suspect that possibly happened the night of her death, as she didn't want anyone to interfere with the heart share."

Tanelith nodded. While she hadn't noticed any of the carvings taking off into the night—she had been preoccupied with other things—but that didn't mean it hadn't happened. Or that Loba hadn't done it that afternoon, while Tanelith had been sleeping.

"But back to the issue at hand, how you will notify me, directly, if you have need?" Adas said. His eyes took on a far off look as he thought.

"Yes," he said after a few moments. "This will do."

He took what looked like a red silk handkerchief out of an inner pocket of his cape. A scalloped edge had been embroidered around it, done with black thread. The work was exquisite, finer than any Tanelith had ever seen.

"Burn this when you need to contact me," he said as he handed it to her.

"What?" Tanelith asked, surprised. She'd expected to be able to throw it on the wind or something else equally romantic.

Or perhaps that would be what Adas claimed had happened, when telling the tale of her epic battles.

"I will feel the destruction of this work," Adas said solemnly. "This cloth holds many secrets. If you sleep with it under your pillow, you may be able to hear me whispering in your dreams. But possibly not—it might be only another Meerimec would."

Tanelith nodded, slipping the cool cloth between her fingers. Loba had said that she couldn't really influence Tanelith's dreams, though they'd been in the same room.

"Why don't you give it to Vyncis?" Tanelith asked.

Adas gave her a sad smile. "He wouldn't listen," he said. "He never has."

Before Tanelith could ask more about that, Vyncis stood walked up to the top of the stairs. "It is time," he said. "We go to bury the body so that it might be renewed."

"We will speak more later," Adas promised.

Tanelith nodded and went to stand at the foot of the stairs while Vyncis directed everyone. Adas, Mira, Lirelli, and Phera (Loba's other sister, the one whose name Tanelith kept forgetting) would carry the body. Vyncis would lead the way.

After they had gathered up the body, the group stepped back and away from Loba's house, waiting. Vyncis held up his hand. As he lowered it, mists gathered over the house, transforming it back into an empty shell that wouldn't admit anyone without need.

While Mira might still want to burn the place down, Tanelith knew that Adas and possibly Vyncis' cousin Aldira might come and look in on the place while they were gone. Plus, it was likely that the house had other defenses.

Tanelith went to stand beside Vyncis, her pack on her back.

He paused for a moment. Was he saying goodbye? Tanelith had no idea when either of them would return here, if they ever would.

"The first step," he said quietly to her, "is always the hardest. Come," he said, reaching out his hand to her.

Tanelith took his solid hand in hers. It was surprisingly strong and calloused, and much warmer than her naturally cool skin.

They took a step together. And the world changed.

TEN

Tanelith hadn't been sure what to expect when Vyncis had said that she'd travel with him, that he'd help her travel as fast as the rest of them.

She remembered being a child, with her father cocooning the entire family together and flying on a beam of moonlight over the grass. Despite the wind, it had always felt warm, all of them together, wrapped up in her father's love.

This travel didn't have that feeling at all. Instead of flying, they were still walking. Or hopping. Or something like that. A small motion...that ended up moving them a great amount.

It was if they had started standing next to one tree, then with a single step, had traveled much of the way through the woods, to a tree in the far distance.

Tanelith's stomach lurched, unused to such travel. She staggered, her feet trying to find solid ground again. Sweat broke out across her temples and down her back.

Vyncis kept a tight hold of her hand. "Ye can do it," he told her firmly.

Tanelith shook her head, trying to clear it. "Are you sure?"

He gave her a grin. "The next one's easier."

Tanelith swallowed down the bile in her throat, grit her teeth, then squeezed Vyncis' hand. "Do it," she said.

Nothing happened.

"Ye have to take a step first," came the laughing voice from beside her.

Tanelith did *not* want to take that next step.

She knew she had to.

It was much like the rest of her life.

She forced her foot off the ground, and stepped.

This time was slightly better. Instead of her stomach objecting so strenuously, she felt as dizzy as if she'd held her breath for a long time, or perhaps spun around fast in a circle. Her knees felt weak, and she locked them so she wouldn't fall down. The trees in front of her were wavy, as if she viewed them from behind wet glass. The air smelled strangely of smoke though there wasn't a fire anywhere near them.

It took her a few moments of gulping air like a drowned person before Tanelith finally nodded to Vyncis, ready to take the next step.

Like the first, this one upset her stomach and made her breakout in a sweat. Her head was more clear, though, and she didn't have as much bile in the back of her throat.

Thankfully, she saw guardian trees just ahead. They were on the border between the normal woods and the huge trunks that lined the edges.

"Is this good enough?" she asked. She had to clear her throat to make herself heard over a whisper.

"It is," Vyncis said. "The others will join us here. Come."

The first few steps after that were annoyingly difficult. Her feet didn't want to shuffle along or leave the ground. It wasn't pain so much as her muscles didn't want to cooperate. She remembered walking through the market place in Faburh with her heels bloodied by blisters. That had been harder, or so she told herself. She could do this.

Walking on the soft mat of leaves helped clear Tanelith's head.

Slowly, the steps grew easier, and her vertigo calmed down. Still, she was glad when they stopped.

A huge tree reared up in front of her. Its roots were spread wide, making a natural bed in front of it. The other Meerimec joined them, stepping out from behind trees and solemnly walking through the woods.

Tanelith had nearly stopped shaking by the time the others reached them.

"Bad, eh?" Adas asked sympathetically.

"I'm here," Tanelith said, as if that put an end to all the discussion.

Because while it had been bad—and she adamantly did *not* want to do that again—she'd made it.

And she'd do it again, for a longer stretch of time, if she had to, if her travels demanded it.

Loba's body, still in its cream-colored shroud, was laid at the foot of the great tree.

Tanelith was surprised that there were no priests or priestesses conducting the final service for Loba. It appeared to be an intimate affair, just family and friends present.

She knew that the Meerimec had priests as well as priestesses. However, none of the Meerimec priests or priestesses had a specific god or goddess. They believed in the dual nature of all things, so they believed in both Celionael as well as the Hidden One, the light and dark forces. The Sun God Gehor and the Rain Goddess Kanoress. The God Zanargil who lived in the mountains and the Goddess Baramunz who lived in the valleys.

Maybe with so many gods, it was difficult to get a priest or priestess to attend a funeral. Tanelith would have to ask later.

First, Vyncis went up to the great tree and touched it with his hands. "Oh great guardian, it is the wish of one of ours to be buried at your roots. Her name was Loba, and she loved you the best."

Tanelith wasn't sure if she was imagining it or not, but she thought she heard a sifting noise through the trees, as if a wind high in their branches had suddenly sprang up.

However, the tree didn't move or speak. Vyncis appeared to take that as a sign, and so he took his hands from the tree trunk and nodded to the others.

All the Meerimec formed a circle, holding hands. Vyncis placed Tanelith next to the tree, instructing her to touch it with one hand and to hold his hand with her other. On the other side of the tree, Adas did the same. It made the tree part of the circle.

Tanelith couldn't perform the same type of magic as the Meerimec. She could only lend Vyncis some of her magical strength. She felt the power of these people flow easily around the circle as they focused on the body before them.

A dark spot appeared underneath the body. Tanelith blinked her eyes. No, she wasn't imagining it. The body was now floating as a hole appeared beneath it. Quickly, the hole deepened. Then Loba was slowly lowered in, disappearing.

Tanelith felt tears gathering. She blinked her eyes to clear them, as she couldn't use her hands to wipe them away.

The hole rapidly refilled, until just a dark spot remained, where the leaves and debris of the forest had been cleared away. The air smelled of fresh dirt. A calm descended on the woods, the birds falling silent.

A loud groaning noise echoed through the woods. The earth started to shake.

Vyncis grabbed Tanelith's hand and pulled her away from the tree.

The tree which was now moving.

Giant roots emerged from the ground and dragged the enormous tree forward. Branches that had been intertwined with its neighboring trees snapped. Limbs came crashing down.

The violent movement only lasted a few moments. Once the tree was in its new location—sprouting directly on top of where the body had been buried—the woods went quiet again. Nothing marked where the tree had been. The earth there had been flattened out, and the usual forest debris covered it.

Tanelith looked at Vyncis, who was staring with wide eyes at the tree trunk beside her.

"The color has changed," Adas announced. "It's grown darker. More red."

Mira opened her mouth to disagree. Her daughter tugged hard on her hand, making sure that she didn't.

"You're right. The color has changed," Phera said. "Look, you can see all the trunks changing."

Tanelith watched. It looked like a wet mist blowing through the woods. Each trunk that it passed turned darker, as if a rain had passed by.

"The guardians have been renewed," Adas said. "They have accepted Loba, as they did the great hero Heobo. Her blood is now shared by all the trees."

Tanelith shivered. She had never thought she'd see an actual legend in the making.

Then again, what was she about to do, but to go on a quest to find the gods?

"The guardians will be stronger, now, more aware," Adas continued. "They have been strengthened for the coming storm."

He looked directly at Tanelith when he said that.

Lirelli and the others all stepped back from her. Even Vyncis.

"I bring no storm," Tanelith protested. "I just want to free my people. So that I have no fear of my children being stolen and turned into slaves."

"Every breath you take brings us closer to war," Lirelli denounced. "I will have no part of it."

With that, she turned and walked away, disappearing as she stepped beside one of the trees.

Surprisingly, Mira stepped forward. "I don't like ye, or yer fancy ways. But ye shouldn't be slaves. No one should have that fear." She turned and looked at Adas. "Let me know when the time arrives."

Adas looked at the rest of the remaining group. A couple of the dozen or so who remained shook their heads and disappeared.

The rest nodded, pledging their allegiance to some future alliance. Aldira and a few others came over to say goodbye to Vyncis before walking away, disappearing as they stepped away, next to the trees.

Finally, all that remained were Adas, Vyncis, and Tanelith.

"I know we've had our differences," Adas said in that soothing voice of his. "But I've always been on your side. When you have need, call."

Tanelith could tell that Vyncis wanted to deny his sire. He didn't want Adas's help. Grudgingly, he nodded. "I will," he said, the words sounding forced.

"I will see to building your grandmother's legend," Adas added with a smug smile. "Her name will become as famous as Heobo's. And, sometime, as yours."

"Mine?" Vyncis said with a scowl.

"You shared her memories. You can become as great as her. Or even greater," Adas said.

Vyncis shook his head. "No. I failed when I tried to travel as she did."

"You'll need to travel as you're supposed to, not as she did," Adas said gently. "I have faith in you, Son."

Vyncis nodded, but Tanelith could tell that he wasn't listening.

"Until we meet again," Adas said. He took a step backwards, then a second, then disappeared.

It was only Tanelith and Vyncis standing in the quiet of the woods. Birds had started chirping again. She heard the rustling of mice in the grass nearby. A soft wind caressed her cheeks, ruffled her short hair.

She adjusted the pack on her back. The dagger stuck up on one side, within easy reach. They had a few days' worth of food, but they could forage along the way, at least while they were in the woods.

She looked expectantly at Vyncis.

He stared at her crossly. "What?" he said.

She shrugged. "You're the guide. Where do we go next?"

"Out of the woods," he said, still clearly upset. "Then, south. And east." He stared at her for a moment. "You know why Loba did this? Why she wanted to renew the trees?"

"No?" Tanelith said. "I mean, I don't believe all of Adas's dire warnings about a war. Or I don't want to believe them."

Vyncis nodded. "The real reason was me. If I fail this mission, if I fail *you*, she'll know. And she won't let me come back home." He was nearly in tears at the admission. "I'm not like Loba. Not really. All the time I was away all I wanted to do was to come back home. To be here in the woods. She's made that impossible. Until you succeed. Or fail."

"No," Tanelith said, shaking her head. "Your mission is only to guide me to the Stairs of the Gods. That's it. You don't have to be involved in the rest of the war if you don't want to be."

He gave a weak laugh. "Believe what you want. But Loba could be cruel. And I need to help you *succeed*." He shook his head and said, "Let's go."

Tanelith waited while Vyncis walked past her, then she followed along behind. She was a little surprised that they weren't flitting from tree to tree again. Maybe Vyncis was tired from the travel that morning, from using his magic to bury his grandmother.

Or maybe he just wanted to spend as much time as he could here in the woods. Before they started their journey, and the woods would close to him until they were finished.

CHAPTER

ELEVEN

Tanelith knew that on her own, it would have taken two or possibly three days to reach the edge of the guardian trees.

However, with Vyncis, it took a single day. She wasn't sure if he'd used a short cut, or if the trees just made it easier for them. They camped that night just inside the last ring of trees. In the morning, they'd be starting across open fields again.

Close to the Human territory. Where slavers would be seeking her.

They quietly made camp that night. Tanelith was surprised when Vyncis lit a fire, though they were still in among the trees. Perhaps the trees didn't mind him doing it. She'd been certain they would have objected if she had.

Then again, she wasn't one of the Meerimec.

Tanelith was glad for one more night in the woods, with the trees protecting them. That night, it was the dark of the moon, when her magic was weakest. They'd start traveling in more open areas when her strength was waxing. Hopefully they wouldn't need it.

Vyncis had caught a few fish which were now sizzling in the coals, wrapped in thick river grass.

They hadn't said much to each other as twilight came and

went. True darkness now crept in. The crackling of the fire was the loudest thing Tanelith heard, though every now and again she heard the rustling of grass as some small creature made their way through. It had gotten colder all day as they'd walked. The tree cover was too thick for her to see the clouds that she was certain covered the sky. They might be walking out into a snow storm, or through snow for their first few days.

Vyncis cleared his throat to get her attention, then finally said, "I've been thinking about how we're going to travel across the Ilburh lands."

Tanelith merely nodded at him to tell him to go on. She, too, had been wondering about that.

"You are an Elf," he said. "There are no free Elves in the Ilburh lands. Only slaves. The best way for us to hide is for you to pretend to be a slave again."

"No," Tanelith said immediately. She shivered to her core. The smell of the cooking fish was suddenly revolting. "I cannot."

"But—"

"No," Tanelith said. "Besides, it wouldn't be safer."

"No one would look at you, or think twice about you being there," Vyncis said. "I could make you a collar. It wouldn't be real. There would be an illusion on it, so that everyone would think it was real."

"And what happens the first time someone raises a pain wand and I don't respond?" Tanelith said. "You don't understand. Being a slave makes me more vulnerable. Any of the Ilburh could decide to order me to do something. Or," she paused, swallowing down the bile that burned at the back of her throats, "one of the Ilburh could decide that I was fit for stud farm."

Vyncis looked at her, shocked. "They couldn't just take you. Not from me."

"You're not my master," Tanelith said bitterly. "You'd be merely a slaver, and not even Gilukkhaz. They certainly could just take me. Use me. They wouldn't really be spoiling the goods, now, would they?"

She trembled, both afraid and angry, as well as mad at herself that she was afraid at all. "I cannot do that again. Never."

Vyncis opened his mouth to protest, then let all the air out of his lungs with a heavy sigh. "All right then. We can't pretend you're a slave. How then, do you propose we cross through Ilburh country?"

"We travel at night," Tanelith said. "We stick to the outskirts, never going into a town."

Vyncis shook his head. "We'll need supplies. We'll have to go into town sometimes."

"Fine, you can get the supplies," Tanelith said. "Though I survived without doing that, after I'd escaped. I broke into a root cellar and stole food."

Vyncis looked horrified at the thought. "Why would we do that?"

"Because we're hiding," she said. "We don't want people to find us." A little thievery was much better than being captured.

Vyncis chewed the inside of his mouth on one side. "I don't know. Maybe."

They sat in stony silence for a few moments. Tanelith could *not* bend on this. She would never be a slave again. Vyncis had worked for an auction house. Hadn't he seen how horrible it had been for the poor slaves?

Then again, had he really thought of them as people? Or had the slavers indoctrinated him, teaching him to never see the Elves as anything but property?

She remembered when she'd first arrived at Loba's house, how Vyncis wouldn't say her name. She couldn't recall if he'd ever used it.

"What's my name?" she asked suddenly.

He grimaced at her. "Tanelith," he said distinctly. "And yes, we were taught to never call a slave by their name. It was part of their training process."

"Part of how *you* were trained, so that you no longer thought of us as people," Tanelith corrected.

Vyncis sighed again. "It's going to be a lot harder if we're traveling only at night, in secret."

"It's the only way," Tanelith insisted.

Vyncis thought for a moment, then nodded at her. "Fine. We'll spend tomorrow camped here, and not leave the woods until after nightfall. I can't see as well as you can in the dark, but I'm not night blind, not like the Ilburh."

Tanelith nodded. After he'd turned the fish in the coals, she said, "Thank you."

Vyncis grunted but didn't say anything more after that.

Tanelith sighed. She drew her knees up and wrapped her arms around them, hugging herself.

Tomorrow night, then, would be the real start of their journey. She'd have to leave the safety of Gishem Woods. Though the woods weren't her home, they had grown dear to her. Particularly since Loba's blood now ran through the guardians.

She knew she'd always be welcome.

Whether or not Vyncis would be wasn't something she needed to worry about, at least not for now.

CHAPTER

TWELVE

Snow slid down through the trees, floating softly on the morning light. Tanelith would have been delighted by the prettiness of it if she hadn't been aware of just how difficult thick, heavy snow would make their travels.

Still, she broke her fast and had some of the hot tea that Vyncis had already made. He was sitting in the exact same spot he'd been in the night before. Had he not slept?

It made no difference to her. She'd needed the rest. She'd spend much of the day dozing and sleeping, easily making the switch over to spending the rest of the night awake. Hopefully, Vyncis would be able to adjust quickly as well.

Tanelith spent much of the day dreaming, thinking about her family. The next dark of the moon would mark the end of the year. Her people would be celebrating the new year. There would be sweet treats and presents. Her mother might weave them all new hats or scarves. Her father might use some of the old clothes he took in that were too worn to be repaired, and make a patchwork vest or blanket for them.

When would she see them again? She longed for her mother's warmth and quick wit, her father's sly laughter. She missed the twins more than she could have ever imagined.

But maybe she could find the cities of the gods. Maybe she'd be able to take them all up, into the clouds one day, floating above the world. Take them to a place where they'd be safe from the slavers.

As darkness fell, Tanelith stirred herself. They had one last meal of the fish they'd caught, the rest of it smoked and in their packs. Then they set off, Vyncis in the lead.

The edge of the woods was only a few steps away. Tanelith paused with Vyncis, looking out over the field in front of them. It was covered in a heavy snow. At least the clouds had cleared. The sky was velvet black, with bright stars twinkling down. Cold winds blew the top of the snow, sculpting it into frozen waves and ridges.

Nothing moved out there. No sound beyond their own breathing, their breath frozen in the air.

"That's going to be a pain to get across," Tanelith said, to break the tension if nothing else.

Vyncis started. "You're right," he said. He looked out as if seeing it for the first time.

What had he been looking at before?

It was only then that she noticed that he had one hand resting on one of the guardian trees. Had he been talking to them? Saying goodbye to his grandmother one last time?

"Can you walk on top of the snow?" Tanelith asked.

"What? No," Vyncis said. "That's impossible."

Tanelith snorted at him. "It's easy. See?" She leaped out, crossing out of the woods and up onto the snow. She took a few running steps away, then came back halfway. "You should try it," she said coaxingly.

Vyncis looked over his shoulder, back into the woods. She knew his heart was breaking. He'd wanted to travel in his grandmother's footsteps. Or perhaps even his sire's. However, his heart wasn't in traveling, seeing the world. It was too tied to the trees.

"Come on," she said. "Unless you're scared to."

She knew that was a low blow. However, it was something she would have said to motivate her sisters.

"Fine," Vyncis snarled. He stepped out past the edge of the trees. He took one step, then another on top of the snow.

"Huh?" he asked.

With his third step, he sank deeply into the snow. It was at least mid-calf high.

"What the...Did you do that?" he accused her.

"What, make the snow along the edges of the trees, where it's more likely to melt and then freeze, be more solid? No, don't be silly," Tanelith said. She had noticed it, however, as she'd skipped across the top of the snow.

"Fine," he grumbled. He sloughed out to where she was still standing, on top of the snow, supported by her magic.

"There isn't any way you can carry me up there with you, right?" Vyncis said, craning his neck up to see her.

"No," Tanelith said, sinking down. "I can't even maintain it. It's too much effort."

"Thank the gods," Vyncis said. "I don't think I could have stood it if you just skipped across the top of the snow all night long."

She could tell that he wanted to say more, possibly something about how this was why the other peoples hated her kind. They made everything look too easy.

Instead, he looked back over his shoulders, at the trail he'd struck leading from the edge of the woods. "Even a blind tracker would be able to follow us."

"I know," Tanelith said. "Any chance you could call up a wind to blur our tracks?"

"No," Vyncis said. "I could only hide them for a little while. But that would only confuse the eyes. If one of the Gilukkhaz were using a *bilnala*, they wouldn't be confused."

"What's a *bilnala*?" Tanelith asked. "Is it one of their seeking stones?"

"Yeah. Sniffers," Vyncis said. "You've seen one?"

"There's one in my pack," Tanelith admitted. "I stole it from the Ilburh man who'd bought me."

"From your master," Vyncis said.

"He isn't my master," Tanelith ground out. "He is one of the Ilburh. Human. Male. Nothing more. And he's dead."

"You killed him?" Vyncis said, completely shocked.

"I did. If I hadn't, he would have raped me."

Tanelith hadn't realized that a Meerimec could grow so pale. "It...that's disgusting."

"What, that he tried? Or that he wanted to?" Tanelith spat out. "Are you going to blame me for his actions?"

"What? No! Any male who would try to take a female against her will is immediately expelled from his village. Until he does his penance, no village will have him. Who would do something like that? Particularly with one of you?" Vyncis asked.

Tanelith didn't reply, though it seemed that the Meerimec was as disgusted by the attempt as well as that anyone would try to mate with one of the Elves.

She kept her angry words to herself. "I'll break our trail for a while. Then we can trade places. We won't get too far tonight. We will need to make it to the next stand of trees, where we can take cover during the day."

"Agreed," Vyncis said. He gestured for her to lead the way.

Tanelith angrily started walking. It was going to be a very long night. She used her magic to keep herself warm, though the exercise was going to help with that. She wouldn't bother drying herself until they called a break.

In the meanwhile, she was going to have to keep at Vyncis, continue to make him use her name, breaking down that training he'd received that he hadn't even thought about, getting him to see her as a person again, and not as an animal or property.

Or even, gods forbid, just an instrument of fate.

CHAPTER

THIRTEEN

When the night was almost over, and they were close to their destination, it started snowing again. Tanelith groaned at the sight. Great. It meant the next night's walk was going to be even more difficult, through thicker banks of snow.

They had been lucky. There had been long patches where the snow had melted and frozen again, with a much thicker crust, so Vyncis as well as Tanelith could walk on top of the mounds for a while.

They hadn't talked much all night, instead, saving their strength and their breath for the difficult walk.

With the new snow, it was going to be twice as hard. Snow would probably come down all day, judging by the clouds they had above them.

"Sun blast this snow," Tanelith cursed as they neared the trees. It was falling harder now, in big thick globes that made it difficult to see.

"You should think of it as a blessing," Vyncis said.

"What?" Tanelith asked. She was hungry, hot, and tired. She didn't want to fight with the Meerimec again.

"It will obliterate the trail we made coming out of the woods," he said. He seemed more at peace with himself than he'd been when they'd started.

"Fine. I guess," Tanelith said, well aware that she sounded like one of her bratty sisters.

"I'll break the path the rest of the way," Vyncis said, walking past her.

Tanelith trudged after him to the stand of tree up ahead. They were mostly pines, not the type that were spread out, but the sort that grew close together, almost on top of one another.

The snow under the branches wasn't anywhere near as thick. Plus, the falling snow had abated.

"What now?" Vyncis asked.

"Sleep," Tanelith said. She was more tired than she wanted to admit.

"Where?" he asked, sounding cautious.

"Up in one of the trees," she said, confused. Where did he think they were going to sleep? Not on the ground, that was for certain.

"Ah," he said. A true smile crossed his face. "You mean, up here?"

Quicker than Tanelith could take a breath, Vyncis was all the way up one of the trees.

"Something like that, yes," Tanelith said. She took her time climbing her own tree, next to the one Vyncis had claimed. Then she wove together a few of the branches to make herself a nest to lay on.

Vyncis' eyes grew wide at that. "How did you do that? I thought only the Meerimec could do that."

Tanelith shrugged. "I've always been able to do this. Some of my friends could do it too." She remembered spending a lazy summer afternoon, up in a tree with some of her girlfriends, above the Dorwine river, lounging in a nest like this. "I'm sure it isn't as fine as yours," she added when she looked over at his own nest.

Hers was flimsy and flat. It would support her weight, but that was about it.

Vyncis' nest was more like a hammock, with sides to keep him from falling out.

"You'll have to teach me how to do that sometime," she said as she used her magic to finally, *finally* get her feet warm and dry.

"And you'll have to teach me how to do that," he commented.

"What?" Tanelith said, horrified. "You can't get yourself warm yourself? Dry out your clothes and your skin?"

Shamefaced, Vyncis shook his head.

"Get over here," Tanelith ordered, "so that I can get you warm and dry. I'll teach you how to do it another time."

"All right," Vyncis said. He appeared to just walk along the tops of the branches between the trees, as if they were solid ground.

Tanelith shook her head. Had he always had that ability? Or had that been a gift of Loba's as well?

After Tanelith had dried Vyncis' clothing and warmed his skin, she showed him the basics of it. As she suspected, he could do it perfectly fine on his own, but no one had taught him how.

When had she learned? Was it because of Olin? Had he mentioned in passing that had been something that the people of the past had done, and so she'd taught herself? She knew her parents mainly relied on the stove and the fireplace to keep the shop and their house warm.

Were the other members of her family able to warm themselves? She wasn't sure.

Vyncis stayed where he was for a little longer, shoring up the sides of Tanelith's nest. The branches seemed to weave themselves together. She knew she'd never be as fast as him when it came to this.

However, she was grateful that he was willing to show her.

Just before he left, Vyncis grew still for a moment, looking out over the field they'd left behind. It was just a white blur beyond the dark tree limbs.

"Trouble doesn't ever come alone," he said softly. "I could never predict a storm or a fire. Trouble always comes with someone. A person. We won't meet any people tomorrow, or possibly the next day as well. After that, there might be trouble."

"And we'll handle it then," Tanelith said softly. "For now, let's get some sleep."

He gave her a sweet smile. "Aye, yer right." He nodded and gracefully climbed out of her nest, across the tree branches to his own.

Despite her exhaustion, Tanelith still took a while falling asleep.

She knew that trouble was on its way. It always was looming on the horizon, as soon as she set foot outside of Gishem Woods.

Whatever it was, though, it wouldn't stop her.

She would set her people free.

FOURTEEN

The following day was much like the first, the pair of them taking turns pounding down a path through the snow. Like the first night, the sky was clear of clouds. A sliver of the moon shone down on them, filling Tanelith with delight as well as renewing her magic.

She wasn't certain, but she suspected that being in the trees helped Vyncis renew his magic. He had certainly seemed stronger and more capable that morning.

That night, before they left, Tanelith told Vyncis about her encounter with the slavers, how she'd disabled their carts, killed their beasts.

How Ugmas had silently promised that he would kill her.

Vyncis sat in stony silence for a few moments, staring out from their current nests in the trees. He'd built her a nest that morning, and she had to admit it was so much more comfortable than anything she'd been able to create for herself.

It reminded her of being a little girl, and how hard her mother had worked at trying to get her to weave something, anything. But her weft and waft were never straight, she was always getting the shuttle tangled in the threads. She just didn't think that way.

She suspected weaving herself a nest tapped into the same

skill. She could do an adequate job, but she really needed to leave it to someone who was talented to do it well.

The stony silence continued. Had Vyncis known Ugmas? She hoped the ugly slaver hadn't been a mentor to him or something equally ridiculous.

"So you destroyed two slaver carts. Stranded four masters of the slave trade. Killed their oxen. Basically, making fools of them. Do I have that right?" Vyncis said, his voice hard.

"Yes," Tanelith said, her chin coming up stubbornly. "And I'd do it again in a heartbeat if I had to."

Vyncis slowly turned his face to her, a grin spreading across it. "They're gonna hate you. They're *all* going to make it their personal vendetta to bring your head back on a platter."

Tanelith stared at Vyncis defiantly. "So?"

He gave a wry laugh and shook his head. "You're right. It doesn't really matter. And perhaps you were right about not trying to pretend to be a slave. They might be checking all slaves, to make sure that no one had captured you accidentally." He sighed. "We'll keep going your way. Traveling at night as we cross the Ilburh lands. I would like to go into a town at some point, to see if I can get any news."

Tanelith nodded. "Do you know where?"

Vyncis shook his head. "Loba's memories are still jumbled. Plus, it's been years since she passed this way. And never in such snow. I have about as much of an idea of where we are as you do. I won't really know until we get out of this valley, and can see some landmarks."

Tanelith nodded slowly. She'd hoped for better news, but she'd still take what she had.

"What was it like?" she asked softly. "Sharing all of Loba's memories?"

Vyncis grimaced. "It was as magical as you might imagine, as well as much less so, at the same time. I know Loba, all of Loba, now. I know things that a grandson shouldn't know about his grandmother. Intimate things."

"Oh," Tanelith said. She hadn't thought of that. She'd assumed that Loba would just share would be the travel bits.

"It's all right. She did some amazing things," Vyncis said. Then he added with a grin, "As well as some incredibly stupid ones. I got to see her both as a young girl, and as a grown woman."

Tanelith nodded.

"I don't have all her memories," Vyncis said after a few moments. "There are some she didn't share. And I don't want to know some of those things. Like just how close she might have been with Adas."

Tanelith shivered. That was...icky. Then again, they were both free spirits. And Vyncis didn't appear to have the same distaste she did for his sire sleeping with both his mother as well as his grandmother.

"Who is Adas?" Tanelith asked. "I mean, besides your sire."

"He's a traveling bard," Vyncis said. "He has no real home. He travels from village to town with news and stories. You should hear him play his lute. And the stories he tells...you just hang onto every word." He gave a bitter laugh. "I couldn't live up to him, either."

"I doubt anyone could," Tanelith said. "Even the storytellers of the Egarlorsar would have stiff competition from him."

"Yeah," Vyncis said. "We should get going."

"Will there be trouble tonight?" Tanelith asked.

Vyncis shrugged. "We're in unclaimed land right now," he said. "Sometime tonight, we'll cross a border, and be in Ilburh territory. I doubt that the Gilukkhaz have set up a patrol there, waiting for you to come out of the woods. It's been months since you fled. But we'll have to be more careful. I'm hoping that we'll run out of snow soon."

They had been heading directly south. It would turn warmer eventually. Tanelith was looking forward to that.

"All right," Tanelith said. She followed Vyncis out of the trees, down to the floor of the grove they were in. The trees had hidden them all day, as well as the clouds.

When they walked out toward the fields, they saw it was snowing again, big fat flakes.

Tanelith sighed. It was going to be another long night. But she would rather spend the night walking and not meet anyone than having to flee for her life.

She still wasn't sure if she could completely trust Vyncis. He ran hot and cold. It was as if he sometimes saw her as a slave, and sometimes as a person.

She wished Loba could have shared her memories with her. That way, Tanelith wouldn't have to rely on anyone else.

Then again, if she was raising an army to fight in a war, she would have to learn how to rely on others. She couldn't fight everyone herself.

She wasn't a god. And even the gods, in the end, had failed.

FIFTEEN

By the end of the night, the falling snow had changed from snow into rain. The snow at their feet was starting to melt, making it easier to walk. Tanelith used a touch of magic to keep her head dry, looking out from the hood of her cloak. She didn't bother with the rest of herself. They'd be dry soon enough.

Vyncis paused just before dawn, looking out over the field in front of them, then to the left and the right. They had taken the easier route, through the grass, particularly while it was still snowing. To the east of them, more pastures and open planes lay. To the west were occasional groves of trees and underbrush. Far beyond the woods stood tall mountains, the Kharakin range that ended with the huge mountain Nyramukz, the homeland of the Dwarves.

"Let's get to the trees," he said. "Now." He started to run, moving more quickly than Tanelith would have thought.

But she was much taller than he was, and had longer legs. In addition, though she was tired, she could travel over the grass with her magic.

She raced up to him, holding the edges of her cloak out as well as her magic. She swept him up beside her as she passed him, lifting his feet off the ground. They flew over to the trees, where she set them both down.

"How did you do that? Never mind," Vyncis said. "Hide. Quickly."

Vyncis stepped next to a tree and disappeared. Tanelith grabbed hold of a shadow and stepped into it.

Nothing happened. She strained her ears and her eyes looking for something out on the plane, where they'd been walking.

She was just about to ask Vyncis what he'd seen when a clanking noise came to her, carried on the wind.

The sound of the chains a slaver carried on their cart.

Tanelith froze in fear. What were slavers doing here? Were they chasing her? Had they already caught her scent? There was no place she could hide if they were tracking her that way.

The carts—all four of them—didn't slow down as they passed, making their way from the south to the north.

Where were they going? Why were there so many of them? She shivered watching them pass. At least Vyncis had been able to warn the pair of them, and they could get to safety quickly.

When she'd been captured, the carts had traveled both day and night, the oxen changed out when they'd grown tired. Were these carts doing that as well? Had they traveled all night? Or had they just gotten an early start, as dawn was starting to streak across the sky?

After the carts had passed, Tanelith stayed where she was, hiding, her breath ragged and her heart beating hard.

She kept asking the question over and over again. What were they going to do?

Eventually, Vyncis stepped out from behind a tree. "Tanelith?" he called softly. "Where are you?"

Tanelith took a deep breath. It was a relief to her that Vyncis couldn't see her, didn't know where she was. She stepped out of the shadows.

"Huh," was all he said when he saw her.

"Who were those slavers? Where were they going?" Tanelith asked.

He shrugged. "I'm not sure." He paused, thinking for a few moments. "You said...you said that the people of the Broken Mountains give up some of their children, yes?"

Tanelith swallowed against a suddenly dry throat. "Yes," she said. She hadn't asked too many questions about the ceremony, afraid that she might grow angry enough to draw her sword and just kill everyone.

She'd assumed that it would happen sometime during the spring.

What if it didn't? What if it happened at New Year's instead?

The slavers would be a bit early, though. The New Year was almost a month away.

Vyncis replied as if he was reading her thoughts. "They can't go through Gishem Woods. Chances are, they'll have to detour widely around it now. Wider than before. So it's going to take them time to get to the Broken Mountains. Longer than usual, I'd suspect."

"Ah," Tanelith said, nodding.

So on the night when everyone else was celebrating, mothers and fathers would be kissing their children goodbye? And they'd probably be forced to put on a brave face for their neighbors, too, pretending as if their hearts weren't breaking.

Tanelith shook her head. She couldn't imagine how bitter some of those adults must feel, having to give up their children.

Or maybe they wouldn't. Maybe they'd choose to leave as well.

Only to be captured by the slavers, possibly before they even made it down to the foothills of the mountain.

She *had* to stop those damned slavers. But how? Even with two people, it would be difficult. Still, there had to be something she could do to save the children. At least this year.

She turned to Vyncis and said, "I'm going after them. You wait here."

Then she sprinted off, moving as fast as the wind.

It would be daylight soon. The clouds were already starting to turn pink.

She wouldn't have much time. But she couldn't let those slave carts continue.

CHAPTER

SIXTEEN

Tanelith found that by using her magic she could easily catch up with the fast trotting oxen. The Goddess seemed to be smiling on her, though, because they stopped after just a short while.

There really wasn't anywhere to hide. The carts had stopped in the middle of a field. Tanelith raced up to them, stealing what shadows she could to disappear into. She drew her dagger, but didn't elongate it into its full length. Instead, she kept it at the in between form, a short blade the length of her forearm. The handpiece also changed, the metal on the back of her hand rising up into sharp spikes.

Tanelith crouched, listening. The rank stench of the Gilukkhaz rolled her. They stank of rancid grease and bitter metal. She had to swallow against the bile in her throat. It was difficult to be so close to them. Fear made her sweat. It also made her angry.

She hadn't been watching too carefully as the carts had driven past, but now she saw that the carts were different. Two of the carts had four wheels. They were covered over with a hoop of off-white cloth.

It was the type of cart that she'd ridden in, after she'd been kidnapped.

The other two carts only had two wheels. They were for fast travel.

She drew closer to the back of one of the four-wheeled carts. The end of the cloth wasn't tied together, so she figured no one had been kidnapped yet. She poked her head in just to make sure, while being very careful not to touch the cart at all. The wood would be reinforced with blood metal, which would drain away her magic.

So these slavers were on their way somewhere, probably hoping to fill their carts.

She could guess where they were going. To the Broken Mountains. She had to grind her teeth to prevent herself from cursing those people. At least, out loud.

But why had the slavers stopped?

The Gilukkhaz had dismounted from their carts, and then had walked in front of them. She wasn't sure what they were doing. When she snuck a look, she understood why.

Snow.

One of the taller, uglier slavers stepped right up to the edge of it. Two others stood just behind him, and the three remaining behind them, creating a triangular formation.

They started to chant. It wasn't the first time that Tanelith had heard their guttural native tongue. It still made her want to retch.

What were they doing?

It took a while for her to figure it out.

Slowly, a dark spot spread out from the feet of the Gilukkhaz who was in front. He slowly stepped forward. The spot stretched at first, growing as wide as a cart. Then it started elongating.

They were melting the snow, creating a path for the carts.

The snow was shrinking back quickly, as if it couldn't bear their touch.

She didn't have much time.

Fortunately, she already knew what she was going to do.

There was nothing in the back of the other covered cart. Six packs rested in one of the two-wheeled carts.

The other held the prize she was seeking: A wooden box that took up the width of the cart, but was only a forearm tall and deep.

Tanelith used her magic to lift the box silently from its resting place, then she sprinted away, carrying it with her. It was heavy. She had to use her magic to help her lift it, as well as to steady it, so that her escape was silent.

Though destroying the four carts would have been satisfying, it also would have been like holding up a large sign with an arrow pointing directly at her, since she had already destroyed two of their carts with her sword.

Now, though, the slavers wouldn't be able to say for certain who had stolen all their food and cooking supplies. They might even blame it on a passing Meerimec.

Likely, they'd accuse her anyway. But as the carts were left intact, they wouldn't be able to say for certain.

Hopefully, the Goddess would continue to smile on her and they'd drive away, not realizing the theft until they stopped again at midday to eat.

By the time Tanelith reached the spot where Vyncis still waited, the exhilaration had deserted her and she was exhausted. They'd traveled all night, and she'd just burned up what little reserves she had.

Tanelith didn't see Vyncis when she plunged into the clearing. She set the box down and straightened up in time to see him stepping out from beside a tree.

"What did you do?" he said sourly. "It was dangerous for you to just go off that way."

Tanelith didn't say the first thing that came to her, though it took her a moment to call the words back.

Accusing Vyncis of sounding like his mother probably wouldn't have a positive outcome.

"I stole all their food," Tanelith said. She couldn't help but giggle at the shocked look on Vyncis' face. "They'd stopped to clear a path through the snow." She sobered at that. She'd seen the Gilukkhaz make a path for their oxen and their carts across rough terrain, raising a flat surface in front of them then smoothing it out behind. Now, she'd seen them digging a road through the snow.

They would be unstoppable if they decided to come after you. Unless you had raised up a barrier like Gishem Woods.

"We can't stay here," Vyncis said. "We'll have to keep moving, to stay ahead of them."

"Why?" Tanelith asked. "How are they going to track a box of food?"

Vyncis opened his mouth then shut it again. "Their sense of smell is very keen," he said after a few moments. "They might be able to smell it."

Tanelith sighed. She was already so tired. "Then we'll take what we want, leave the rest here, and travel onward to the next grove of trees. They won't be able to find us there."

"It would be safer to keep going," Vyncis said slowly. "How about we travel until midday, then rest? That at least puts more distance between us and this." He gestured at the unopened box that lay between them, as if it were a rotting Ilburh corpse.

"We did need food," Tanelith pointed out as she crouched down to open the box.

"I am not a thief," Vyncis ground out.

"Well, you might want to rethink that," Tanelith shot back as she started digging out the dried meat and hard cheese she found. "Because you're traveling with an escaped slave who wants to kill each and every slaver she finds."

"Even me?" Vyncis said angrily.

Tanelith sat back on her heels and looked up at him. "At first? Yes. The only reason you're still alive is because Loba said that you'd given up being a slaver."

Vyncis looked away, chewing on his lips as if biting back all the words he wanted to say.

Finally, he looked back at Tanelith. "You're right," he said more softly. "I am paying my penance. Loba declared that I couldn't be both a Meerimec and a slaver. I chose my home. Which I've now been forced out of."

"Don't you think I miss my home?" Tanelith snapped, still angry. "Miss my family? But there's a bigger cause out here. An injustice that needs righting. I can't just hide my head in the sand, hoping for the trouble to pass me by. It's coming. The slavers are coming for my people And I have to stop them."

"You can't save them all," Vyncis said. He sounded angry again.

"I can try," Tanelith said, glaring at him.

After a few long moments, Vyncis finally nodded. "I know. And I will help."

He walked over next to her and started riffling through the box of supplies.

Once both of their packs were full, Tanelith stood. Her leg muscles groaned and her head swam with exhaustion.

Still, she would keep going, despite the fact that they were going to be traveling during the day, under the sun, which was so much more difficult for her.

She placed her pack on her back without complaint, ready to go as far that day as they had to, until Vyncis declared them safe.

He gave her a broad wink, then turned back to the wooden trunk. "Burying the trunk won't do any good. The Gilukkhaz are good with the earth. I can't hide it either. They'd be able to sniff their way through any illusion. However, if I do this…"

Vyncis slowly lifted his hands. The trunk followed, floating up. Then Vyncis made a strong pushing motion, wedging the trunk into the limbs of the large leaf maple tree.

"They'll have quite a time getting it down from there," he told her with a grin. "The tree won't like it. It will fight them in little ways, like raining twigs and leaves down on them. It's too big around for them to be able to chop it down. Their magic won't work on it. They'll know that they're after a Meerimec, not one of the Egarlorsar."

His grin fell away. "I used to look up to them, you know. They were brave in the face of any danger. Strong. Independent. They care deeply about their families." He paused, then added, "And they hate the Egarlorsar with every fiber of their being."

Tanelith nodded. She didn't know what her people had done to offend the Gilukkhaz so deeply. They must have very different stories about the War of Betrayal.

"Let's go," Tanelith said after a moment. "But also, Vyncis? Thank you."

Vyncis gave her a single nod, then took off across the field.

Tanelith followed, glad that they were out of the rain and the snow, though they were not out of trouble. Not by a long shot.

CHAPTER

SEVENTEEN

The days and nights flowed one into another. Tanelith grew stronger as the full moon approached. They were heading more east than south now, and were deep in the heart of Ilburh country.

The rain had followed them, for which Tanelith was grateful. She'd grown up with rain, listening to it splash against the roof, watching it drip off ivy on ruined walls, smelling the fresh green scent it left behind. She'd been kidnapped during the summer, maybe six months ago now, then in Faburh all fall when there was no rain. She'd missed it. Even though she was tired of walking through it all night, or crouched down with it beating through the trees all day, she still wouldn't wish it away.

Vyncis didn't appear to relish it as much as she did. However, he was getting much better at drying his own socks and cloak, as well as keeping himself warm without a fire.

Tanelith did miss hot tea. Hot food as well. But they couldn't risk a fire. Even with the rain there would be some smoke, easily seen in such flat, open country.

They'd replenished their supplies, or rather, Tanelith had, breaking into the root cellar of a farm now and again. Sometimes she pulled down shelves and tore sausages apart, trying to make it

93

look like an animal attack. Other times, she only stole a few items, stored at the back of full shelves, so that perhaps no one would miss what she'd taken, at least not for some time.

Vyncis still flat refused to come with her on her raids. It was too dangerous, according to him. He would, however, gratefully eat anything Tanelith provided for them.

"Why are you so against thieves?" Tanelith finally asked one evening after she'd brought back a large cured ham, several well-cured sausages, as well as a surprisingly large bag of dried walnuts.

Vyncis chewed thoughtfully for a moment. "The Meerimec—it's considered a serious crime among us. The penance for stealing is always very arduous."

Tanelith nodded. "I get that. But you seem particularly appalled by it."

"I think it was my time in Haedun," he said after a bit. "The Ilburh, while they consider stealing a crime, it isn't as serious. That's how the beggars get away with it." He sighed. "When you ask me to steal something, I found myself wanting to say that I wasn't an Ilburh beggar."

"Why do the Humans allow the beggars to exist?" Tanelith said. "Why don't they take care of their own people?" It was something that had always bewildered her. Sometimes people needed help. If they needed help too often, the temple would often send someone to work with them, to bring them back into the ways of the Elves. She'd heard that the problem was often grief. A husband would lose his wife or his child and no longer want to work. A woman would not be able to get pregnant and would stop working.

"I think there weren't always beggars," Vyncis said slowly. "They're just starting to have slaves in their society. It cheapens them all, as a result."

Tanelith sighed and nodded. She didn't know if ending the slave trade would help the Ilburh. There was a part of her that didn't want to help them in the least.

However, it would be better if all lives were valued, not just those who were rich and well-off.

After they finished eating, Tanelith turned to go climb one of the pines they were camped beneath. However, Vyncis stayed where he was.

"Aren't you going to rest?" Tanelith asked before she started up. They hadn't traveled as far that night as usual because of her theft. The morning would be arriving soon. She could smell it on the air. The rains had stopped for now, though she figured her luck wouldn't last for too long, and that by mid-morning she'd wake up to find water dripping on her face.

"I'm going into Darcot," he announced. "That's the name of the closest town. It's south of Faburh. I'll buy us some supplies, and hear what news there is."

"What news do you hope to hear?" Tanelith asked, confused.

"Those slavers who you stole from must have made it back into town by now," Vyncis said. "I'd like to hear what stories they have, who they think is to blame. And to see what plans they have to hunt you."

Tanelith sighed. She really didn't like the thought of Vyncis going into town on his own. If she was completely honest with herself, she feared that he'd turn her in.

Being a Meerimec was important to him, though. And hopefully, she'd opened his eyes at least a little, so he'd see exactly what the slave trade really was.

"And what do I do if you don't come back?" Tanelith finally asked quietly.

"I'll come back," Vyncis said. "I have to see that your mission is successful. Remember?"

She sighed. "I don't like it."

He gave her a huge grin. "Now, you sound like me, every time you go off to steal from a root cellar."

"I know," Tanelith said. "What should I do if you don't come back?" she repeated stubbornly.

"Come and rescue me," Vyncis said. "No one is going to be able to stop you, not with that sword and armor."

Tanelith nodded. She still didn't like it. However, she knew that Vyncis would be careful. And some more food, maybe even some fresh bread, would be lovely.

"All right," she said after a few moments. "You go into town today. But I expect you back here by sundown."

Vyncis shook his head. "I'll need to eat supper with them. I won't be able to head out until after dark."

"Them?" Tanelith asked. Did he have friends in Darcot who he'd forgotten to mention?

Vyncis nodded. He reached for his pack and rooted around in it, finally pulling something out of the very bottom of it.

His slaver's vest.

Tanelith couldn't help herself. At least she turned her head before she spat. "A plague on all slavers," she growled. "You've been intending this the entire time, going into town and pretending to still be one of them."

Vyncis blinked slowly, then nodded. "Yes. Remember? I had originally planned on you pretending to be a slave. Of course I carried the vest with me."

"Oh," Tanelith said, her anger abating. "Right. I remember, now." She'd been so upset she'd forgotten his original plan.

Hers was better. She knew that, and hopefully, he did as well by now.

"I'll be back before midnight," he said as he stripped off his regular shirt. He shivered as he drew the vest back on.

For the first time, Tanelith noticed a triangular scar on Vyncis' left shoulder. It looked too precise for a wound. "What's that?" she asked, pointing.

Vyncis looked down at the spot, then looked away.

"It was how one of the Meerimec proved themselves to the Gilukkhaz. By bearing their brand." He looked back at his scar as if fascinated by it, though still disgusted at the same time. He ran cautious fingers across it, then shook his head. "They made it with a blood metal knife. I didn't learn that until later. It could have killed me."

He looked straight at Tanelith. "By marking me, they hoped to separate me from my people. That being so marked, my people would turn away from me. Maybe they hoped that some of the blood metal would remain, soaked into my blood. I don't know." He shook his head. "The Meerimec don't understand what this mark is. They don't know. Or at least my family didn't. People in the bigger towns might recognize it."

"Did Loba know?" Tanelith asked.

"Not before she died, no. Or rather, before we started sharing. She learned then. The sharing wasn't all one sided." He sighed. "Why?"

"If she knew, and she accepted you anyway, then she believed your penance would be enough, that the others will accept you as well," Tanelith said.

"It's hard sometimes," Vyncis admitted as he pulled the vest tight across his chest. "I think I hear her talking to me. Even when I'm awake."

"She might be whispering to you," Tanelith said. "I miss her too." She hadn't know the old Meerimec long, but she'd taken a large place in Tanelith's heart, particularly as the first to treat Tanelith as a person after she'd escaped her captors.

Vyncis gave her a grin. "Right now, I think she'd be yelling at me for being an idiot and getting involved with the slavers in the first place."

"She might have a point," Tanelith teased.

Vyncis rolled his eyes at her, then he grew more serious and nodded. "I also think she'd say that some risks are worth taking. And this is one of them. It's a small risk, but it might bring a huge reward."

"Then you should go," Tanelith said. "However, be prepared for a lot of yelling if I end up having to rescue you."

He grinned. "I'll be sure to come back early, then." He sobered then repeated, "I'll be back by midnight."

He stepped next to a tree, then vanished.

Tanelith knew that he couldn't travel as quickly from tree to tree outside of Gishem Woods. Instead of moving a far distance, the next tree always had to be in sight. It could be a good ways off, as long as it was still visible.

Tanelith climbed the tree she'd chosen for the rest of the day, hauling both her pack and Vyncis' up with her. The nest she wove for herself was perfectly adequate, though nowhere near as good as one the Meerimec could build.

It surprised her when she fell asleep right away. She must have been more tired than she'd realized.

It did not surprise her in the least when midnight came and went and there was no sign of Vyncis.

EIGHTEEN

Tanelith changed trees before morning came, though she stayed in the same grove. While moving might make it more difficult for Vyncis to find her, it would also make it harder for anyone else.

She spent the day restless, coming up with horrific scenarios. He'd been recognized by someone as an escaped Meerimec. Or someone else had placed her and him together. She tried to rest as well as she could.

As soon as twilight came, Tanelith started preparing herself. She ate and drank sparingly. She kept both her pack as well as Vyncis in the new nest she'd made, up in the trees.

The only thing she took with her was the dagger. Truly, it would be all she needed.

At least it was night. Tanelith flowed through the shadows, keeping herself as hidden as possible.

The town of Darcot was in a valley. Instead of going directly to it, she climbed one of the nearby hills to look down on it.

Like most everything the Ilburh touched, there was a sense of order to the structure. The town was almost a perfect circle, with straight streets crossing each other on a grid.

It looked so sterile to her, particularly when she remembered the winding streets of her village, how they curved to match the banks of the Dorwine.

As she'd feared, there was a wall built all the way around the town. Fortunately, it wasn't that tall. It worked with the magic in the blood metal collars the slaves wore, making it impossible for them to escape.

She knew that the Dissolving Blade could destroy that wall. And if she could, she would smite it. But she couldn't.

Not yet.

Something Vyncis had said to her struck her again. She could not save them all. No matter how she tried. Some lives were going to be ruined, and people would die enslaved before she could get all her plans in place.

Which just meant she needed to get moving again. Now. Before the night ended and dawn came calling.

Tanelith melted into the shadows as she drew closer to the town. It was so hard to make herself move forward. She stopped just outside of one of the gates, pausing, swaying.

She didn't want to set foot inside another Ilburh town. Not ever. But she was armed this time. Possibly not dangerous, as she still didn't have a good idea how to fight. She'd been reluctant to practice the sword dance in front of Vyncis.

That had to stop. She needed to use the blade regularly if she was to be a warrior.

First, though, she needed to rescue him.

When she'd been in the hills above the town, she thought she'd been able to figure out which part of the town would be the poorer end. It was surprisingly close to one of the gates. However, if Darcot was built like Faburh, that meant it was also the area where the slave auction house would be.

Would Vyncis be there? She didn't know. Or would he have moved to a richer place already?

She refused to believe that he was dead. She just had to hope that he hadn't turned his back on her, that he really did want to fulfill Loba's penitence.

Tanelith made herself crouch down after a few more moments of not moving, of not seeing anyone on the far side of the gate, she finally raced through the opening of the wall. She doubted that there would be a gong ringing someplace else in town, alerting anyone to her presence.

The people of the Broken Mountains had that magic. The Ilburh did not, she was certain.

As Tanelith had suspected, the auction house for the slaves was close to the poorer part of town. She recognized the carts of the Gilukkhaz. Though she itched to destroy every single one of them, she held back. She hadn't bothered to transform the Dissolving Blade yet: she carried it in its ceremonial form.

Would the blade stay hidden in the shadows if it was glowing? Would she? She was going to have to work with Vyncis to make sure that the shadows would still hide her if she was fully armed.

Rough laughter came from one of the buildings. Tanelith slowly snuck up to one of the windows.

Human buildings were poorly constructed, particularly compared to the Egarlorsar or Meerimec. They used straight boards that didn't meld into one another, so there were gaps, stuffed full of mud or plaster.

This section of town was also poorer, so the buildings were even rougher.

However, at least for this building, the window panes held glass.

Slowly, Tanelith poked her head up, gazing inside the room.

The room was well lit from magical fires burning in sconces hanging from the walls. The light was cheery, and she could tell it was warm inside. Ten people sat around a large table. They appeared to be playing a card game. A pile of red markers sat heaped in the middle of the table.

All of the people were slavers. They all wore the vest of their office.

Nine of them were Gilukkhaz. But there was one person who was shorter. With curly brown hair.

Vyncis.

He hadn't been captured or killed. No, he'd chosen to stay with the slavers. Given up his Meerimec ways.

Tanelith's heart pounded loud in her ears when Vyncis suddenly looked directly at her.

Could he see her? How? She was hidden by shadows.

He threw down the cards he was holding in disgust and said something that made the others laugh. Then he stood up from the table, stretched, and walked out the door of the room.

Tanelith hurried toward the door of the building, certain that was where Vyncis was going.

She stayed hidden, watching as he sort of staggered across the yard, between one building and the next.

Then—she couldn't believe what she saw.

He was going to urinate against the wall he was facing!

Vyncis, who was so squeamish about her stealing. She just couldn't believe it.

"Tomorrow."

She heard the word over the sound of urine splashing against the wall.

Suddenly, one of the other slavers came barreling out the door. The wood slapped hard against the plaster, making her jump.

"Eh, there ye are," he called roughly.

He saw what Vyncis was doing, and gave a barking laugh. "That's what I told me boys yer were. Ha!"

"Where did you think I was going?" Vyncis asked as he finished up.

"Eh, ye know. They're a might twitchy these days 'bout yer kind." The Gilukkhaz came to stand beside Vyncis and took himself out.

Tanelith couldn't believe that he, too, was going to just urinate on the wall.

Perhaps it was the edge of the slave quarters. That would

make sense, that they'd want to degrade her people as much as they could.

"I know," Vyncis said with a sigh. "Believe me, I know."

"Ye need a new crew, say the word," the Gilukkhaz said. "Could use a hard worker."

"Thank you," Vyncis said. He sounded sincere. "But I have to get back to my crew tomorrow."

"Yer loyalty's worth more than ye know," the slaver said. He threw an arm over Vyncis' shoulders. "Come on. Time to git back t' the others."

Vyncis nodded and walked with the slaver, never turning to look for Tanelith.

They walked into the building and the door shut, the sound of the others' laughter abruptly cut off.

What was going on? Vyncis wasn't being held against his will. But he had whispered the word, "Tomorrow." And he'd just told that slaver that he needed to get back to his crew tomorrow as well.

Tanelith sighed. She'd been all ready for a grand fight, to break Vyncis out of a jail or worse, a slave pen.

Seemed that he needed to break himself out, though.

Tanelith turned and raced back out of Darcot as quickly as her magic would take her.

Tomorrow would be the reckoning. Not tonight.

Tonight, she'd practice her sword dancing while trying to hide in shadows. Just so she would be prepared for whatever happened next.

NINETEEN

It was mid-morning when Vyncis stepped out from beside one of the trees in the grove where Tanelith was staying. He stayed perfectly still where he was, with his empty hands held out a little by his sides.

She stayed where she was in the shadows, her sword drawn and ready.

When no one else appeared, finally Tanelith said, "What happened?"

Tanelith immediately stepped into a different shadow, moving quickly, so that he wouldn't be able to track her by her voice. Vyncis kept his eyes staring right in front of him, not trying to find her.

"Do you remember that box of food we stole? That I then put up in the crook of a tree?" Vyncis asked.

Tanelith nodded, then remembered he couldn't see her. "I do," she said. Then she quickly moved to another spot, so that he couldn't find her.

Vyncis continued, his gaze straight ahead. "It worked too well. The Gilukkhaz were already paranoid because of you. Now, they believe that the Meerimec might have turned against them. I had to stay to prove my loyalty by staying an extra day. If I hadn't, they would have started chasing me as well. And they had my scent. They would have found us."

Tanelith didn't want to believe him. However, she knew that it would be better if the slavers weren't trying to track both of them.

"All right," she said, keeping to the shadows. She did step closer to him. "What else did you learn?"

"I want to show you something," Vyncis said. He moved his right hand slowly toward the pocket of his vest, then pulled out a scroll of paper. "Here."

He held the scroll out, then dropped it.

Tanelith caught it before it fell, stepping out of the shadows as she did.

There was a drawing done of her at the top of the page. It was actually quite a good likeness.

Below was the offer of a huge reward—twice what she'd been worth as a slave—for her return.

To Arryn. In Faburh.

"What does this mean?" Tanelith said, bewildered.

"You didn't kill your old master," Vyncis said grimly. "You merely injured him. They say that his left arm is withered, and he can't use it."

Tanelith couldn't remember what she'd done besides sticking the monster behind her with the Dissolving Blade, just as he'd been about to rape her.

Had she just skewered him, and not actually killed him? He'd lain so still on the floor, the blood pooling around him.

Or had he been playing possum, so that she'd leave and he could heal himself?

She didn't know. She didn't think he'd had that cool of a head. No, he'd been unconscious. Somehow, he'd woken up and saved himself.

Maybe the boy had heard something, and he'd come down to find his father lying on the floor.

She wouldn't have wished that on Rudrick, no matter how badly his father had treated her.

"I...I don't know," Tanelith said finally. "I really thought I'd killed him."

A part of her was stupidly glad that she hadn't actually killed anyone.

Another part of her was disgusted that that *animal* was still alive.

"I know," Vyncis said softly. "That reward makes it more likely that the Gilukkhaz coming after us will not kill you. Unless it's Ugmas and his crew."

"What about Ugmas?" Tanelith said, suddenly warry.

"He doesn't know where that sword came from," Vyncis said, with a nod to the blade. "But he's certain it's a warning. And he'll tell anyone who will listen to him about how this is the start of the bad times. How the Gilukkhaz should raid every Egarlorsar village and town, to take you all into slavery now. Kill anyone who isn't willing to wear the collar."

Tanelith shivered. She hadn't imagined that would be the consequence of her initial battle with Ugmas and the other slavers, when she destroyed their carts and butchered their oxen.

"Don't worry," Vyncis said. "At this time, no one is listening to him. They think he's crazy, going after you that way. You're only one slave. What can you do?"

"But now they're afraid of the Meerimec," she said as she released the blade in her hand, prompting it to go back to its ceremonial disguise.

"And the trees of Gishem Woods are decidedly less friendly than they've ever been," Vyncis said. He sighed. "Fortunately, the Meerimec make lousy slaves. Or I think they'd be trying to figure out how to raid the woods."

Tanelith nodded. She was suddenly very happy that Loba had renewed the guardian trees, making it more difficult for anyone with ill intent to breach the trees.

"Still, all Meerimec are suspect, at this point. And slavers always travel as a crew. Always. It's very rare that a slaver works alone." Vyncis grimaced. "I knew that, but I'd forgotten. They were doubly suspicious of me when I arrived in town alone."

"So what happened?" Tanelith asked, realizing that she'd already asked that question once.

"When I arrived, I had a story about this wild attack. How we'd woken up and the cart wheels had been cut in half. They were more than happy to believe it," Vyncis said, a small smile crossing his face. "They knew about the Meerimec ability to cross long distances using trees," he said. He shook his head. "I'd always wondered why there were so few trees in an Ilburh town. And even less, I'm told, in Gilukkhaz ones."

"That's why?" Tanelith said, surprised, though she'd also wondered the same thing. It was as if every family could have their single tree in their yard, but only the richer families. In the poorer parts of Faburh, no trees had survived.

"Maybe, yes," Vyncis said. "So they believed me about how I got separated from my crew. But then they wouldn't let me leave to go back to them. Said they should have sent someone with me. They called my crew all kinds of names for letting me come alone."

"Huh," Tanelith said. She'd had no idea. When she thought back to seeing slavers in Faburh, she had always seen them together, as a group. Never singly.

"They let me go back, though, after I'd spent two nights there. I'm not sure why they thought that would make me less of a spy," he said.

"Was it so that way they could get a better hold of your scent? So they could follow you here?" Tanelith asked.

"I'd wondered about that, but I don't think so. I left at dawn this morning. I've been wandering up and down, through the hills and back, just so they would have difficulty tracking me here."

"We should still leave. Now," Tanelith said. She was tired, and she knew that Vyncis was tired.

However, Vyncis just nodded. "I had figured that might be what we decided." He gave her a smile, then showed her the small pack he'd been wearing, that he hadn't worn before. "Full of food, for a crew of four," he promised her.

"Good," Tanelith said. "Wait here."

She went to the tree where she'd spent part of the night and morning, climbing up it rapidly to fetch down both of their packs.

"Thanks for believing me," Vyncis said as she handed his pack to him. He took off the smaller pack, then attached it to the outside of his larger pack.

Tanelith only then noticed the odd patch on the side of the small pack. It was an off-shade of yellow against the plain brown of the canvas pack, in the shape of a small triangle, maybe two fingers across.

"What's that?" she asked. She reached out and ran a finger across it, then shuddered.

There was blood metal—just the smallest amount—woven into it.

"What's what?" Vyncis said. He took off his pack and stared at the small patch. "I didn't know that was there," he said. He looked up at her horrified. "They can track me with that."

Tanelith shuddered. "They kept you there to lull you, so that you wouldn't be suspicious of them," she said accusingly. "Now, they're hunting you."

"I don't want to leave this here," Vyncis said, looking around wildly. "We need to get rid of it, though. Quickly."

"We need to dump the food," Tanelith instructed. "Then you take the bag, leave it up on one of the hills surrounding the town. They'll be able to find it fairly quickly, but it won't lead them here."

Tanelith upended the bag and dumped all the food out onto the beaten down grass under the trees. Then she took it by a strap and shoved it at him.

Vyncis stood there, mouth gaping.

"Go!" Tanelith ordered.

"I'm so sorry," he said. He took the strap and ran toward the first tree, disappearing as he stepped beside it.

There had been good bread in the pack, which Tanelith was loath to leave behind. A wheel of hard cheese as well. Some dried meat and a jar of what looked like honey.

She touched everything, even sticking her finger into the honey and swishing it around, seeking anywhere else that the damned slavers might have stuck a tracking patch, or even a thread of blood metal.

Nothing else appeared to be marked. She stuffed as much as she could carry into her own pack, storing most of the food there, putting the rest of it into Vyncis' pack.

He came back more quickly than she expected. He looked pale. "They're already searching for me," he said. "I'm so sorry. You were right. We shouldn't have gone anywhere near a town."

Tanelith grimaced. "Do they suspect that you're with me?" she asked.

"I don't know. I don't think so," he said. "I don't think they would have let me go if they'd suspected that."

"They might have kept you so that they would see if I would come, using you as bait," Tanelith said.

"Why didn't they hold onto me longer, then?" Vyncis asked as he shouldered his pack.

"I don't know. But they have your scent. We need to run, fast as the wind, for now."

Vyncis nodded. "You're going to have to travel with me for a while," he said. "Stepping trees."

"I know," Tanelith said. She gave him a wry smile. "Good thing I was too wound up to really eat anything this morning."

"Aye," Vyncis acknowledged. "I don't know if it will be easier or harder, doing this outside of Gishem Woods."

"Let's find out," Tanelith said. She held out her hand.

Vyncis took it. His skin was hot, possibly from all the magic he'd been expending. "Hopefully, by this afternoon, they'll have lost the scent."

Tanelith nodded, though she doubted that would happen.

Slavers would mercilessly be tracking them from now on.

Until they found them and killed them.

CHAPTER

TWENTY

Tanelith knew that the first step would be the hardest. But she was determined to move, and keep moving.

They stepped from the grove they were in to a tree not too far away, directly south of where they'd been.

Her head pounded and dots swam in front of her eyes. Her mostly empty stomach clenched and knotted. She forced herself to take a deep breath, swallow, then nod at Vyncis.

They stepped again.

This time, Tanelith felt her throat closing up on her. She gasped, drawing air in. She was sweating hard, as if she'd run the entire distance.

"Keep going," she directed Vyncis.

He looked concerned, but they stepped again.

The next few steps weren't any easier, but luckily, they weren't any more difficult, either. Tanelith found she could suffer through the pain and dizziness.

There were worse things, after all. Like wearing a blood metal collar.

They kept traveling in a fairly straight line, due south. Tanelith panted at each stop, her head swimming, her legs and arms shaking. The edges of her sight darkened, as if she was looking through a tunnel. The bottom of her stomach felt hollow and hard, as if she'd swallowed a huge bubble.

She was afraid that when that bubble burst, she'd vomit all of her insides out.

They kept going, Tanelith determined to endure.

Until finally, she tried to take a step and fell flat on her face, unable to go on anymore.

"Hide yourself," Vyncis said through gritted teeth. "Hide!"

Tanelith managed to keep her groan to herself as she rolled over onto her side, dragging a shadow over her body like a cold, wet blanket.

She gulped the air as though a bag had just been removed from her head. Her sweat cooled as her heart slowed, though it took a while. Where were they? Where was Vyncis?

Groggily, Tanelith sat up. At least she had the sense to keep her shadow wrapped tightly around her.

They had landed at the back of a grove of birch trees that faced a road.

A party of slavers stood on the other side of the road, taking a break.

Tanelith froze, horrified.

Were there slaves in those covered carts? She couldn't tell from here. Couldn't hear the whimpering of the women or the groans of the men.

Perhaps the lead slaver wasn't as bad as Ugmas, who'd tortured them just so he could have his "music."

Tanelith shuddered but stayed where she was, recovering from the ordeal of traveling as hard as they had. It had weakened her, tremendously. It would take quite a while before her hands stopped shaking and her insides settled down.

However, she also remembered traveling at the back of one of those carts, of being helpless and terrified. The blood metal draining away all magic, all hope.

Without making a sound, she mouthed the names of all those who had endured with her. Findelye. Indimal. Miryelle. She would never forget them. If she could, she would rescue them today from the places they were now enslaved.

She couldn't save them all, though.

Even if she'd wanted to go and attack the carts in front of her, she had no strength left. Just remaining in the shadows was taking everything out of her.

Bitterly, she watched the slavers finish their meal, then start down the road again.

Vyncis stepped out from behind a tree behind her. "I'm sorry. That was too close."

Tanelith nodded. They couldn't just step from tree to tree blindly. Who knew where they might end up?

"It's all right," she said as she slowly stood up. Every muscle and joint ached, as if she'd been in a battle and beaten half to death. She swayed for a moment before forcing herself upright.

"We should continue," she said through gritted teeth.

"No, we shouldn't," Vyncis said. He gave her a wry smile. "I kind of wish I'd kept that patch, though."

"What? Why?" Tanelith said, shocked.

"I could have put it on one of those carts," he said. "Or maybe you could have. Let the slavers hunt their own."

Tanelith had to smile at that. "You're right," she said. "That would have been something."

She took a deep breath, trying to prepare herself for the next tree step that they took. Her arm trembled as she tried to force herself to hold out her hand to Vyncis, so they could keep going.

She was ashamed at how hard her hand shook, but she stubbornly extended it.

"I think we should stay here for the rest of the day," Vyncis said gently, pushing her hand down. "While I can go tree stepping all day long, bringing someone with me takes a lot of magic. More than I'd thought it would."

Tanelith nodded, relieved that they didn't have to go again, at least not right away.

Then she looked up at the tree beside her and groaned. She did *not* want to have to climb a tree right now. She was too tired.

"This way," Vyncis said after a few moments.

Tanelith nodded and followed along after him. After taking a few steps, it was as if her feet found the ground again and her head cleared significantly. She was still exhausted, but her body hurt less.

She wasn't sure how Vyncis had found such a large grove of trees,, all of them bushy elms with soft leaves hiding their trunks. However, she was grateful that he had. He walked them away from the road, until they were hidden on the far side of the elms and undergrowth, the road no longer visible when she looked back. "You can rest here, on the ground for a while," he said. "I'll keep watch."

"Are you sure?" Tanelith said. "I thought I was supposed to stand guard," she added, trying for a teasing tone but possibly missing given Vyncis' lack of a smile in response.

Chances were, she sounded like one of her bratty sisters.

"It's all right," Vyncis said. "I can do it this once. Rest."

Tanelith nodded. She hadn't wanted to fall asleep propped up against a tree, but she couldn't help herself.

She kept her blade in her hand the entire time, just in case.

She jerked awake, the sound of chains clanging against a cart chasing her from her dreams into her waking life.

"It's all right," Vyncis said. "They're passing by on the road behind us," he warned.

Tanelith nodded. She *hated* that sound. The slavers used it deliberately to cause fear, she knew.

She stayed where she was, waiting for the sound to diminish and disappear on the road behind them. The tree she leaned against smelled of musty lichen and good dirt. Birds chirped above her, and she heard the flurry of nearby wings. The air was still in the hot afternoon. Tanelith was suddenly grateful for the shade, as the sunlight would drain her even more than she already was.

Vyncis stood beside her, his face scrunched together as he thought hard. "The road behind us is a border road," he said slowly. "It marks the edge of the Ilburh territory. They're only on this side, the north side of the road. The south side marks the edge of the desert. It's unclaimed territory, except for a few ranches and farms, and a couple of towns as well. But the desert isn't really populated. It's too harsh of a climate, too hard to live there."

Tanelith nodded, her thoughts finally stringing together again. "You should change clothes," she said. All right, given how slowly she was speaking, maybe she wasn't as recovered as she thought she was.

Vyncis looked down at his slaver's vest with distaste. "I'd thought about it. But I left it on so that we could have this discussion."

"If they no longer trust the Meerimec, if they put a tracker on the pack they gave you, you can't be found wearing it again. You can't even keep it with you. They can't find it on you, if we're ever taken," Tanelith said, happy that she was managing to sound more energetic than she was.

Vyncis made a face. "I know. I was just thinking it might be good to leave it some place symbolic. Like maybe at the back of a slaver's cart."

Tanelith thought for a few moments. "No," she said. "It's too risky. We have to leave it."

"They'll know we came this way, if I just abandon it here," Vyncis said.

"All right, we'll carry it with us for a while," Tanelith said, giving in. "Where's the nearest river?"

Vyncis scrunched his face together again as he thought. "Behind us," he said after a few moments. "There won't be much more than ponds up ahead. We'll be in the desert, soon."

"All right. But maybe we leave it behind in a watering hole, after we make sure your scent is well and truly washed from it," she said as she pushed herself upright.

"Where are you going?" Vyncis said as she looked around. "I thought we'd stay here for the rest of the day."

"I can't," Tanelith said. "Not with those slavers passing by. I can't stand the sound of the chains. And I know I can't save them all, but I sure want to destroy every cart I see."

"All right," Vyncis said. "However, I can't step through many more trees. According to my memories, once you get south of the border road, there isn't much."

"Let's go, then," Tanelith said, holding out her hand.

"Are you sure?" Vyncis said. "We should wait and travel tonight."

"Just away from here," Tanelith said.

"Fine," Vyncis said, taking her hand. "But then we rest."

"We will," she said.

And she stepped again, because she had to, not because she wanted to.

CHAPTER

TWENTY-ONE

True night brought a chill to the air that Tanelith wasn't expecting.

Once they'd passed south of the border road, the weather had changed. It was like passing through a curtain. On the one side, there was a chance of regular rain.

On the other side, the dry air spoke of never seeing any moisture.

They were camped near an outcrop of rock. There were no trees that they could stay near. No large growths of bushes or smaller plants. There were hills, though. The flatlands of the Ilburh had given way to rolling hills as well as some very steep rocky climbs.

Tanelith and Vyncis had spent the afternoon curled up in the shade, out of the sunlight. While the Elves would burn badly if they spent too long in the sunshine, the Meerimec were more immune. They would still burn, but not as quickly.

The Humans loved the sun. They worshiped it, and the sun God Gehor. Olin's books told tales of how the Ilburh came from the south. As a people, they'd wandered across the desert, away from their homelands, until they came to the green fields and unclaimed territory. It was only then that they met their neighbors, the Meerimec and the Egarlorsar, and eventually, the Gilukkhaz.

Tanelith knew that the Ilburh didn't remember such a tale, or rather, that they didn't believe it. They did believe that their god created them second, after the Egarlorsar. However, Gehor had watched Celionael create her people, noting her mistakes, and then creating a race that was stronger and more perfect.

The night came quickly to the desert. It was as if the sun raced away, eager to drain its heat from the earth.

Tanelith wasn't sure she'd ever seen so many stars peeking out from the night sky before. There were enough to make her dizzy. She had always been taught that the stars were part of the celestial chorus, made up primarily of Egarlorsar who had died, who sang the goddess's praises evermore.

While the sun had been unforgiving in the pale blue sky, the night, while it looked softer, was just as harsh as the cold descended. Tanelith shivered and was forced to use a little of her magic to warm herself.

She didn't want to use much. Traveling with Vyncis, stepping through trees, had drained her severely.

Fortunately, the moon was nearing full. She should be able to refill herself tonight.

They ate cold bread and cheese, drinking from their water flasks. Tanelith had understood that water would become an issue in the desert. It wasn't until she'd actually seen it, stepped onto this broad plane with nothing but the occasional bush, that she'd realized just how much of a problem it could become.

Loba had been right, sharing her memories with Vyncis. Tanelith wouldn't have ever found water here. Not without a guide who knew the way.

"Are you ready to go?" Vyncis asked, stepping up beside her.

"Yes," Tanelith said. She shouldered her pack.

"It's good that we're traveling at night," Vyncis commented as they started to walk. "That was how Loba traveled. It's how most people travel through the desert. You can't walk during the day. It gets too hot. You'll use too much water, too much magic. You can really only travel during the night."

"I see," Tanelith said. That worried her, actually. One of the reasons why they'd traveled during the night was so that they wouldn't see anyone else. If everyone traveled at night, that made it more likely someone might see them.

However, she truly couldn't see traveling during the day. The sun would burn her to a crisp. Her magic would only support her for so long, and she needed to save her strength.

Vyncis had changed into a regular Meerimec shirt. It was cut out of blocks of cloth, not individual pieces that had been tailored to fit the body. It always made them seem more chunky, but also more solid.

The slaver vests were long and lean, meant to make the wearer look taller or something ridiculous like that. The Gilukkhaz couldn't help it. They weren't much taller than the Meerimec.

"Did Loba travel through here?" Tanelith asked after a while.

Vyncis nodded. "Either here, or somewhere near here. She was familiar with Darcot, which had been one of the reasons why I wanted to go there. There are other border towns. But Loba had traveled to Darcot, and skipped the others."

"What is the nearest town on this side of the border?" Tanelith said, curious.

"As I said, there aren't many. I think," he paused, scrunching up his face, "I think Umulund is near."

"That doesn't sound like an Ilburh town," Tanelith said.

"It isn't," Vyncis said with a grimace. "It's a Gilukkhaz town."

Tanelith nodded and thought while they kept walking. "We aren't really going into any more town, are we?"

"Not for a while," Vyncis agreed. "It's too dangerous. Not just for you, but for me as well. We'll have to make do out here."

Tanelith wasn't sure why those words worried her more, but they did.

CHAPTER

TWENTY-TWO

It only took Tanelith a day and a night to recover from the ordeal of stepping through trees with Vyncis. The moon shining down from the clear sky had helped tremendously.

And despite the heat come sunrise, she still slept deeply and heavily through most of the day.

It was evening again. She'd already changed clothes, adding more layers to combat the chill of the night.

Everything here was so different than where she'd grown up, or really, anywhere she'd ever seen before.

Gray-green shrubs dotted the wide plane. The tallest of them reached her waist. Frequently, they had long thorns or blade-like leaves. Instead of flat lands, they were constantly scrambling down one side of a sloping hill, then climbing up the other side. In the daylight, the rocks were mostly yellow or red, with striations of brown thrown in for good measure. The air smelled of sage and baked rock. When a wind kicked up, it swirled the dust around, making it dance like fallen leaves.

Tanelith could see the beauty in this place. It brought a quiet with it, the hush distilling into a stillness that struck deep into her soul.

The Ilburh were too busy to appreciate the tranquility of the

123

desert. She couldn't imagine how powerful one of the Humans might get if he or she could calm down enough to harness that energy.

They hadn't seen another person the entire day. The only animals they'd seen were small lizards, the occasional mouse, and the hawks who spiraled overhead.

"Is there anyone nearby?" Tanelith asked Vyncis as she stood after they'd finished their evening meal. Night was already encroaching, and stars were starting to peek out of the sky. The smell of the baking rocks changed, growing thinner with the fading light. The air still wasn't soft against her cheeks—she doubted that would happen until she was someplace where it rained regularly. Still, it wasn't as harsh in the twilight, and wouldn't be until it had transformed into true night and the cold had set in.

Vyncis shook his head. "I doubt it." They hadn't had a fire that evening, but had talked about maybe finding a better rock enclosure the next morning, when they finished their traveling for the night.

"Good," Tanelith said. She took a deep breath, then went to fetch her dagger.

"What are you doing?" Vyncis said. He sounded alarmed.

"Practicing," Tanelith said. "I need to practice with the sword. I'm no warrior. I need to learn how to fight. The sword is teaching me how."

Vyncis didn't say anything, but just watched as Tanelith self-consciously called the armor to herself. It spread readily across her body, even with the extra clothes she was wearing.

She didn't feel any warmer or any colder in the armor, which was too bad. She'd hoped that it would protect her more from the elements. Seemed that its magic was bound up in protection from attack, not snow or sun.

However, it also shone with its own milky-white light, like a beacon on a hill.

"You're too bright, too obvious," Vyncis complained to her.

"Is this better?" she asked, as she pulled a shadow over her.

"Yes," Vyncis said. "I can barely see you now."

"Good," Tanelith said. "Your job is to call out and tell me when I've dropped the shadows by accident."

"I can do that," Vyncis said.

Tanelith took a deep breath, then released it before she held the sword up. She paused for a moment, with her arms raised and both hands wrapped around the pommel of the sword. Would the armor protect her from the sunlight? Possibly. But probably not. She might have to experiment with it at some point.

For now, she bowed her head and let the dance begin.

She moved stiffly at first. It had been weeks since she'd tried to do this.

Pivot. Block. Strike. Step back. Deflect.

She kept her feet on the ground at first. It was one less thing to worry about while she warmed up.

As soon as she left the ground, Vyncis called out, "Too bright."

Tanelith concentrated on the shadows around her, drawing them closer to her.

"Still too bright," Vyncis told her.

Only when Tanelith floated back to the ground did the shadows take proper hold again.

Huh. That was unexpected. Or were shadows tied to the earth some way? She would have to figure that out, too, later.

In the meanwhile, Tanelith went through the dance of the sword again, this time faster, feeling more confident as the sword led her through the movements of a fight again.

When she finished, she thanked the Goddess for showing her the light, and the Hidden One for keeping her safe. Then she withdrew the armor, shunting it back into the ceremonial dagger and her larger handpiece. It went easily, which was good. That meant that the armor didn't sense an immediate threat to her.

As Tanelith had suspected, using the armor and the sword had made her more tired than she'd like. However, since the moon was almost full, she assumed that she'd regain her strength as they walked, refilling her magic with the moonlight.

Vyncis nodded at her as she came up to him. "Very pretty," he said dryly, "but you know nothing about fighting."

Tanelith opened her mouth to snap at him, then closed it again. "That's what I was *doing*," she said after a few moments. "I was learning how to fight."

"No, that's not fighting," Vyncis said.

"What do you know about it?" Tanelith huffed.

Vyncis broke out into a large grin. "The Meerimec, well, we don't fight. Not like the Gilukkhaz. We wrestle. And I was always a great wrestler. However, when I was a slaver, the Gilukkhaz taught us how to fight like they do. With their fists and their feet."

"Can you teach me?" Tanelith said. It might be useful to learn how the Gilukkhaz fought.

And more importantly, the Ilburh.

"Put down the dagger and let me show you some things," Vyncis said.

Tanelith placed the dagger next to her pack, close enough that she could call it if she needed.

Vyncis came and stood in front of her, studying her. Not her face, but her torso.

A lightning fast hand struck her abdomen.

The blow didn't hurt, but it did surprise her. Tanelith knew, *knew* she should be able to block such a strike before it reached her. However, she didn't think of that until afterward.

Though the blow wasn't hard, she still staggered back a step. "Ow," she said.

Vyncis nodded grimly at her. "That's what I suspected," he said. "You know the moves, but you have no idea how to apply any of them."

Tanelith tried not to get angry at that. It was actually an accurate assessment. "Then what do you propose?" she said, trying not to sound hurt or resentful.

"Let's start slow. But we need to do this every night," Vyncis said seriously. "You have to learn how to really fight. Not just with a sword, but also with your fists and your feet."

He punched her again. This time, though, he moved slowly.

Tanelith brought her arm down, catching his wrist with her forearm and sweeping it to the side before he could strike her.

"See? That's what you need to do. Think about what each of those movements you're doing with the sword are actually for, why you are learning it, what it's purpose is, then start applying them," Vyncis said. "These moves must become instinctive."

They practiced for a while, always moving slowly, with Vyncis throwing punches that she blocked, then Tanelith had the chance to throw a few punches that Vyncis easily pushed away.

"Why are you doing this?" Tanelith asked after they'd finished and were getting set to start that night's journey.

Vyncis settled his pack more firmly on his back. "Grandmother didn't just want me to lead you to the Stairs of the Gods. She wanted me to make sure that you *won*. That you were successful in whatever you were trying to do. Learning how to fight...that's just going to make you more successful."

"Thank you," Tanelith said. She hadn't imagined that Vyncis was going to be any more than just a guide through the desert.

It turned out, he was so much more.

CHAPTER
TWENTY-THREE

Just as dawn was sending blazing colors across the wide sky, Tanelith spotted two rabbits up ahead.

"You see that?" she said softly, pointing the pair of bunnies out to Vyncis.

They weren't like the rabbits she knew from around Alath. Here, they were long and lean, their fur a yellowish-dust color instead of brown or gray.

"Dinner," Vyncis replied. He stooped and picked up two sharp rocks near his feet. Almost faster than she could see, he hurled the first toward the rabbits, hitting one squarely in its head. Before the other one could scurry away, a second rock joined the first. It hit the rabbit in the back.

Tanelith raced across the light-colored rocks and wrung the necks of the two animals, as much to put them out of any pain as for anything else, as neither blow had killed them.

"This is what we'll be having for a while, now," Vyncis said as he reached for the animals. "Whatever we can catch and kill."

Tanelith nodded. She'd been aware that the desert was going to be a rough place for them to travel. She really hadn't known just how tough it was going to be.

Once again, she was grateful for Vyncis as her guide. They

spitted the rabbits, letting them cook slowly all day while they slept through the heat.

That night, Tanelith said, "You were really, really fast with that stone." She'd been impressed with how accurately he'd thrown the rock and struck the rabbits, and had been thinking about it most of the day when she hadn't been sleeping.

Vyncis gave her a grin. "It's something you should probably know about the Meerimec. We're really good with throwing stones and such. We can hit pretty much anything we aim at, if it's close enough."

"That's good to know," Tanelith said. She paused, then figured she should ask anyway, as she might need the information later. "If it turns out I am leading an army of the Meerimec, what other things should I think about?"

Vyncis looked at her, puzzled. Then he sighed. "Adas. That's who you're talking about. Isn't it."

"He did say that he'd spoken with a lot of young people. People who didn't think that the world ended at the edge of Gishem Woods," Tanelith replied, feeling slightly defensive.

"I wouldn't necessarily count on Adas for anything," Vyncis warned. "He may have a few people he could call on. Then again, it might only be a few. Not an army's worth."

"All right. Message received. He might exaggerate some," Tanelith said. Which made sense, given that his chosen profession was *storyteller*. "Still, what would a few of the Meerimec contribute to an army? Powers that are uniquely theirs?"

Vyncis looked away for a moment. The way his face kind of scrunched up told her that he was consulting his memories, the ones that he'd gotten from Loba. Finally, he nodded and turned back to her.

"Loba trusted you," he said. "More so than I think almost any other Meerimec would. We're taught from an early age to not trust, to stay hidden, to not get involved with the bigger folk outside the woods."

Tanelith wanted to ask how Vyncis had overcome that to

work with the slavers, but decided that would be a conversation for another time.

"So I'm going to trust you as well. A lot of what I tell you, well, I doubt that anyone else knows. Anyone who isn't a Meerimec," Vyncis said.

"I will honor your trust, and not tell another soul," Tanelith said. She paused, then added, "When I left Loba at the edge of the woods, before I went to the Broken Mountains, she talked about how the trees would sing her home," she said. "She sprinted up into one of the guardians, then leaped between them, moving faster through the trees than anyone could on the ground, with all those roots."

Vyncis nodded. "Yes, she shared that memory, as part of showing me that she trusted you."

"I have never told anyone about what Loba did," Tanelith said. "Not any of the other Egarlorsar that I met up in the Broken Mountains. I only vaguely talked about meeting a Meerimec. I never gave them Loba's name, never told them about her house either, how she disguised it."

That earned her a big smile. "Good," Vyncis said. "Because that's one of the advantages of the Meerimec. We can make you see things that aren't there. Or not see them, which can sometimes be just as important."

"So what would you do if you were facing an army of the Gilukkhaz? Or the Ilburh?" Tanelith asked.

"Me? Run away as fast as I could," Vyncis said with a grin. Then he sobered. "If I was somehow protected, I could raise what would look like rolling fog or a dust storm. Blind the other army. That way, you could get very close without them seeing you. I could also throw creatures at them who weren't real. Maybe a swarm of bees to sting them, distract them while your army attacked. Or a collection of snakes." He gave a shudder at that.

"Are you afraid of snakes?" Tanelith asked. Every evening when they'd stopped, Vyncis had always checked the rocks carefully, making sure there weren't any critters who might slip out of the cracks.

Vyncis nodded, eyes wide. "I've always had nightmares about them."

"Then why did you carve a snake? At Loba's house?" Tanelith said. She still remembered the fight she'd had with one.

"That was me gran's idea," Vyncis said with a grimace. "To draw out some of the fear. Didn't work." He paused, then said, "I hadn't thought about it before. But that snake wasn't there after the funeral. I'd assumed that someone had taken it, thinking that it was one of Loba's pieces."

Tanelith shook her head and told him about the night she'd spent protecting the sleepers, how she'd had to at first fight a snake, then a dark tree, then finally, confronting Ugmas.

Vyncis nodded slowly. "The snake was mine. That was my greatest fear. The tree must have been Loba's." He thought for a moment. "Yes. That was hers. An evil tree, who was determined to attack people instead of protect them."

"Was any of it real?" Tanelith had to ask.

"I don't know," Vyncis said with a shrug. "Loba doesn't really know either. It was as much of a test as anything else. To see if you could combat not only someone else's fear, but your own."

Tanelith nodded. If she thought about it in terms of leading an army, that made sense. She'd have to deal with other people's fears, not just her own.

"We should get going," she said after a few moments.

"Yeah," Vyncis said. "Just keep an eye out for snakes, all right?"

"I will," Tanelith said with a grin. Then she sobered. "And we both need to watch for slavers."

Just because they hadn't seen them recently didn't mean they weren't somewhere behind, stalking after them.

CHAPTER

TWENTY-FOUR

They made it a full week before they heard the distinct clanking of chains behind them. The moon was waning, and Tanelith's strength was already low.

Had the slavers come across their trail? Or were they just searching for any elf nearby?

The sound of the chains echoed clearly behind them, across the empty hills. Dawn was a short while away, though Tanelith could already feel the way the world changed, as if the rocks perked up at the approach of the sun. The air was still cool, but the musty smell of the sand and the peppery smell of the sagebush was growing with the dawn.

She glanced over at Vyncis, who nodded grimly. It wasn't a waking dream, a nightmare that had followed her. He'd heard it too.

Slavers.

There were no handy outcroppings of rock nearby. They were heading downhill, another of the steep slopes that filled this land. Near the bottom, they'd hoped to find water to refill their flagons and enough shade to rest in for the day. The hill they were climbing down faced the east. They'd be exposed by the sun soon enough.

"Run," Vyncis whispered, taking off at full speed down the hill.

Tanelith followed after him, cursing the slavers. She didn't know how far away they were. Unfortunately, if they were close, the trail Vyncis and she left would be easy to follow, as they kicked up the dust with their feet that remained visible for a while.

Vyncis led them straight down. Tanelith had to rely on what little magic she had remaining to stay upright and not topple over on the steep slope. When he was almost to the bottom of the ravine, he veered off, running across the face of the hill.

Where was he going? It took a few moments before Tanelith saw what he'd seen, what looked like an outcropping of rock along the side.

But it was just a jumble of rocks, one piled up on top of another. There didn't appear to be an easy entrance, or a place to escape to. Plus, since they were at the bottom of the ravine, when the sunlight struck, it would be focused on them. It would be far too warm for them to spend the day here.

Still, Tanelith followed, scrambling up one set of rocks, then another, after Vyncis. She scraped the palms of her hand and broke off yet another fingernail as she made her way up one boulder, leaping off the far side, landing hard despite the touch of magic she'd used to control her fall.

Finally, they reached the top of the rock pile. It was strangely smooth, as if it had been pounded flat by many feet over the ages. Looking straight across the even plane, Tanelith didn't see anything. It was only when she followed directly behind Vyncis, to the side, that she saw a dark recess, hidden by a standing rock.

Before Vyncis could make it halfway across the flat area, a voice called out, "Stop! Who goes there?"

A figure appeared, stepping out of the shadows beside the stones.

It was an Ilburh woman. Her silver, curly hair glinted in the rising sunlight, while her skin was bronze and leathery from being out in that same light for too long. She wore strange clothes that Tanelith had never seen before. It looked like a coarse blanket woven with many colorful stripes, that the person had merely cut a hole in for her head, then belted around her. She carried a long heavy spear made of black metal. The head was triangular, with three sharp edges that ran to a sharpened point. At least a dozen necklaces hung from her neck, made from leather strips or fraying cord. The charms hanging from them looked rough and weathered.

Tanelith stopped beside Vyncis. "Please," she panted. "We have to hide. Slavers are coming after us!"

"Slavers, eh?" the old woman said. She glared at the pair of them. "I will not thank you for bringing them to my doorstep. But I will deal with them. You may step inside. Don't touch anything until I get back," she warned.

The strange woman whirled away, as if she were made of dust and blown on the wind.

Tanelith and Vyncis looked at each other with wide eyes.

"I have no idea," Vyncis said. "Come. Let's get out of the sunlight."

The sun had just peeked over the edge of the hill. The temperature started climbing immediately.

The dark opening in front of them had changed slightly. Instead of being just a rough hole in the rocks, it looked more deliberate, as if it had been built there.

Slowly, Vyncis and Tanelith walked through the opening.

It was like stepping into a different world.

Inside the cave—or perhaps dwelling would be a better term —the temperature was cool. There appeared to be holes set in the ceiling that let in light, like the skylights that Olin had in his shop. It took Tanelith a moment to place the sound she heard. At the far back of the open area a tiny trickle of water ran into a large holding pool.

Tanelith took a couple of steps further into the room. It wasn't very large, maybe only two-thirds the size of Loba's house.

The dwelling felt as though it was only half-made, while the other half was still natural.

Soft dirt covered the floor. A few oval rugs, braided out of faded white and blue rags, lay scattered here and there. Rough rocks made up the walls. The furniture, what little of it was there, appeared to be made out of carved rocks. But mostly, this place was untamed.

Possibly as wild as its owner.

Tanelith stayed where she was by the doorway. When Vyncis made to go further in, she grabbed his arm and shook her head.

She didn't know why she didn't feel like speaking. But this was a place of deep silence. The only sound it was used to was the quiet echo of the water in the basin on the far wall.

Vyncis nodded and stayed where he was. "Loba had heard of this woman, the wild woman of Tybarh," he said. "But she didn't meet her. She's supposed to be an amazing magician."

Tanelith nodded. She'd remembered thinking how powerful the Ilburh could be in the desert. They had strong fire magic. Even Rudrick could light small fire. Why had the Ilburh moved further north?

"What's her name?" Tanelith asked.

"Rytha," came a voice from behind her.

Tanelith and Vyncis turned. Rytha passed by them brusquely then paused and looked around. "Good. You didn't touch anything. You may stay until evening."

"What about the slavers?" Tanelith asked.

Rytha gave a mirthless chuckle. It sent chills up Tanelith's spine. "They won't be bothering anyone for a while, now," she said. "A massive dust storm sprang up, seemingly out of nowhere. That happens sometimes here. The axle of their cart snapped when they tried to turn it too quickly. Their oxen were drown in the sand."

"Thank you," Tanelith said, her eyes wide.

"I don't abide slavers on my property," Rytha said with a

dismissive sniff. "They know better than to come here. And what I'll do if they return."

She looked at the pair of them. "And who might ye be, this odd pair so deep in the desert?"

"I'm Tanelith, and this is Vyncis," Tanelith said. "We truly appreciate your hospitality."

Rytha peered at her for a moment, her gaze trying to penetrate Tanelith's secrets. Finally, the old woman nodded, then turned and walked further into the open room. "Come," she said. "Sit. I'll make ye some food. Ye can sleep here. But once dusk comes, ye should be gone."

"We will be," Vyncis said. "Thank you," he added.

Rytha set her staff in a holder that was close to the center of the room, where it would be bathed in sunlight, then walked to the right of the holding pool.

Tanelith had thought that there were just more rocks there, that it was the edge of the dwelling. Now, she realized that the rocks were deliberately placed to form a deception. There was another room there. It wasn't a real illusion, like what the Meerimec could do, or what Loba had done with her house. The rocks had just been shaded enough, and it was dim enough, that unless you walked up to the opening of the area, you wouldn't see it.

This dwelling place was a lot larger than she'd first assumed. Maybe it was twice the size of Loba's house.

"Help yourselves to water," Rytha called out as she started assembling a meal for them.

Tanelith cautiously stepped forward. Chambers led off from the main area, darkened tunnels to who knew what. From one she thought she heard the faint sound of chickens clucking.

She and Vyncis took their turns filling flagons with sweet, clean water. She also splashed a little on her face and rinsed off her hands slightly.

Oh, how she longed to stand in the rain! Or even to dip her entire body in a stream.

She was never going to take such luxuries for granted ever again.

Rytha came out of the kitchen area bearing a full platter. It smelled like eggs fried in pork grease, heaped with peppers and onions. She placed it on a low rock table close to her staff, then indicated that they should sit beside her.

Tanelith awkwardly knelt down. The table was at almost the right height for Vyncis but too low for herself. She tried to hunch down, though, to fit in with the others.

Before she served anyone, Rytha sang a hymn. It was in her native Ilburh language, so Tanelith had no idea what she was saying.

When Rytha finished, she switched over to Common and repeated the prayer.

We thank the Sun God Gehor and the Rain Goddess
  Kanoress. Without you, there would be no life.
We thank the God of the mountains, Zanargil for the
  metals we use and the meat we eat, and the Goddess
  Baramunz who lives in the valleys, for the wood and the
  crops.
We thank the Goddess Celionael for the spirit that inhabits
  us all, and her consort the Nameless One, who gives us
  the mysteries and magic.
Alone, we are nothing.
Only with all of you, can we be whole.

Tanelith had never heard of the Hidden One being called the consort of the Goddess before.

She was also quite frankly shocked that any of the Ilburh would even consider Celionael a goddess. She remembered Arryn's dismissive tone when she talked about the ceremonial purposes of the dagger, how unimportant that was to him.

The food was amazing. Tanelith hadn't realized how much she missed all the spices that Rytha had used. It was spicier than

Tanelith was used to—she found herself reaching for her flagon more than once—but it was still hot and fresh.

Rytha served them tea afterward, again, not a variety that Tanelith was used to but having a hot beverage after a meal was a luxury that they'd forgone, particularly as they needed to save their water for their traveling.

"So tell me what brings a Meerimec and an Egarlorsar to my doorstep?" Rytha said. "Surely you haven't just been fleeing the slavers the entire time. What are you running toward?"

Tanelith glanced over at Vyncis, who shrugged. It was up to her how much she told Rytha.

However, Tanelith suspected that like Loba, Rytha lived for the truth, and would know any falsehood she spoke.

"Have you ever heard of the Stairs of the Gods?" Tanelith asked.

Rytha's wild, white eyebrows climbed. "Ohhh. That. So yer running away from the world?"

"What do you mean?" Tanelith asked, instead of instantly denying the Ilburh's accusation.

"I know yer people go there. Make a pilgrimage of it. They never return," she said.

"I will return," Tanelith said stubbornly.

"What makes you so different?" Rytha said dismissively.

Tanelith was tempted to show off a little, maybe grab a shadow and hide. Though Rytha was different, she was still Human, still one of those people.

However, Tanelith didn't try to hide. Instead, she got up and fetched the dagger out of the side of her pack where she'd left it.

She held up the blade for Rytha to see. The old woman looked at it blankly, obviously not recognizing it.

Tanelith dropped a little bit of magic into the blade, coaxing it to extend into its intermediate stage, of a long, sharp blade that was still metal.

Rytha blinked in surprised. She glanced at the blade, then at the handpiece that had also changed, growing spikes.

"Yer one of them warriors. I've heard tales of yer kind," she said. She sounded suspicious.

"My people are being enslaved," Tanelith said, drawing the magic out of the blade and back into herself. The blade went back to its ceremonial form willingly, so she assumed that it didn't view Rytha as a threat.

Which may or may not be true.

"I mean to free them," she added, raising her chin stubbornly.

"The balance has turned, yes," Rytha said. She glared at Tanelith. "Just remember that it was yer people who enslaved the rest first."

"What do you mean?" Tanelith asked. She'd never really understood why the other races despised her people so.

"We were yer slaves, long before ye became ours," Rytha said. "We grew crops for ye, with no hope of fair pay. The Gilukkhaz mined their mountains for ye, hollowing out their sacred spots because ye demanded it."

"We didn't put people in collars that stole away all their magic," Tanelith said. Whatever else her ancestors might be guilty of, that much she was certain of.

Rytha's eyes lingered for a moment on the scar on Tanelith's neck. Then she said, "Ye bound us just the same. Yer magic is so much stronger than any of the others." She held up her hand before Tanelith could object. "The wheel's turned too far. Just as it wasn't right for your people to do that, it isn't right for my people to do what they're doing, either."

Tanelith thought for a moment. "I agree, it isn't right." She sighed. "I need to free my people. But I don't want to enslave your people in order to do it."

That at least got her an honest smile from Rytha. "We'll see if ye can right the balance, at least for a while." She paused. "So ye think that up beyond those stairs, ye might find help? Bring it back?"

"I do," Tanelith said. She paused before she added, "I think the gods still exist. I think they're still floating in their cities above us."

"Then why haven't they reached down to help afore now?" Rytha said. She sounded aggravated.

Tanelith shrugged. "Maybe no one has asked them the right way. Yet."

Rytha laughed at that. "I wish ye luck, that ye have the right combination of pride and humility to talk to those bastards." Then she sobered. "I will not fight ye, if ye come back down with an army. I will not defend my people and what they're doing. Neither will I help you attack them."

"That's about the best I could ask for," Tanelith said honestly. She'd been worried about how Rytha would react to any war that Tanelith might bring.

The silence gathered around them, the natural state of this dwelling. Tanelith tried not to yawn but couldn't help it. She and Vyncis were generally asleep soon after dawn.

"Ye need to rest now," Rytha said. "Ye'll be safe here. I give you my word."

Tanelith knew that Rytha's word was sacred, that breaking the giant staff that stood beside her would be more easily done.

"Thank you," Tanelith said.

Rytha led them down one of the passages to a darkened room. It was half full of supplies, like bags of wheat and corn flour, dried herbs and garlic hanging from the ceiling, cans of pickled vegetables lining the walls.

"It's the best I can do," Rytha said with a shrug. "I don't get many visitors."

"It's great," Vyncis assured her, as did Tanelith.

"We'll speak more at dinner," Rytha said. "Then ye'll be on yer way."

She seemed intent on making sure that they realized that while they were welcome to stay for a short while, they couldn't stay for long.

"Yes," Tanelith said. "We'll be on our way. Thank you."

Rytha gave them a sweet smile. "It's for the best," she said softly. Then she let them be.

While Vyncis was asleep seemingly as soon as he laid down, Tanelith found she still had too many questions about Rytha, the Ilburh, and the past.

Soon, though, she also succumbed to a deep sleep where the fear of the slavers was banished, at least for a while.

CHAPTER

TWENTY-FIVE

Rytha insisted on fixing them dinner, another meal with spicy eggs and vegetables fried together, served with a freshly baked flatbread.

Tanelith kept trying to figure out how to ask Rytha about herself without being rude. Finally, she settled on asking, "Are there many other Ilburh around here?" She figured she could justify the question fairly easily. Every other Ilburh person she'd met had considered her a slave, not a person.

She hadn't realized just how nice it was to have Rytha treat her like someone who was worthwhile and not property.

"No," Rytha said with a sad smile. "It's just me. There are other deep desert dwellers, but we don't talk much to each other."

"What happened to the Ilburh?" Tanelith said. The words poured out of her as soon as she let the first question slip. "They fit here, in the desert. This should be their home. Why did they move north? Do you know?"

"Bits and pieces, handed down through the ages," Rytha said. She sighed and took a large gulp of water. "Now, you'll get a different story from every person you ask. I can only tell you what I know."

Tanelith nodded, as did Vyncis, encouraging Rytha to continue.

"Yer right, the Ilburh used to live in the desert. Not too far from here. The winds and the sands have eaten or buried most of the remains of the ancient cities. Ye can still find traces of them, here and there. A few of the cities still have parts above ground, though." She paused, her eyes looking far away. "The people grew arrogant, as only the Ilburh can." A quick smile flashed across her face before her expression grew darker. "A schism developed when the rains stopped falling."

"You get rain here?" Tanelith asked, surprised. She'd assumed that no water ever came here.

"Aye, in a month or so from now," Rytha said. "I'll wake up one morning and the world will have changed. Everything green and growing like mad." She paused then added, "It's noisy."

Tanelith hadn't ever thought about how a lot of growth might sound, but given the stillness that the desert encouraged, that made sense.

"I've heard the tale both ways, actually. That the rains stopped and a schism developed. Or that a schism developed and the rains stopped. It was so long ago, no one knows for certain. But the people stopped paying attention to all the gods," she said. It was obvious she disapproved of that. "They started saying that only Gehor was important. Kind of like your people, with Celionael."

Tanelith wanted to protest that her people also worshiped the Hidden One, but now wasn't the time. Instead, she merely nodded, to keep Rytha talking.

"The men stopped going to the temple of the Rain Goddess Kanoress. Said she'd betrayed them. They got angry. They wanted the Sun God, Gehor, to force her to bring back the waters." Rytha shook her head. "Can't ever force a woman to do anything. Particularly if she doesn't want to. When the rains next came, they flooded everything. Broke the bridges over the dry river, ruined the fields, destroyed the cities and the roads."

Rytha looked as though she wanted to spit at the thought of it all. "The people might have been able to stay. If they'd humbled themselves. Made themselves go ask their neighbors for help. Instead, they stubbornly left. Gathered up all the men, women and children, and marched them straight across the desert to the softer lands."

"You said there was more than one city," Tanelith said.

"The others died slowly, once most of the people were gone. And the weather became much more erratic. The rains wouldn't come every year. There might be floods when they did come, or barely enough to fill the city's wells. By keeping only a single god, the Ilburh decided their own fate."

Rytha's eyes burned into Tanelith's. "By the Sun God they'll live, and by Him, they'll die. Arrogant to the last."

Tanelith couldn't help the shiver she gave at the doom Rytha pronounced on her own people.

"What happens if Tanelith does turn the wheel? Bring the balance back?" Vyncis asked quietly.

"Eh," Rytha said, leaning back, suddenly a lot less intense. "We'll see, then. I don't know if the northerners will ever come back to the desert, to the old ways. The living was hard. They're softer now, where they are." She paused, then added, "And the Goddess Kanoress has never forgiven them. She still hides her face sometimes when it's most needed. No, I don't think the Ilburh can come back here. They're still going to be your problem."

Tanelith nodded, feeling weighted down by the burden the old person had placed on her shoulders.

Not only did she have to free her people, she had to make sure that the wheel didn't turn too far, that the Elves didn't decide to rise up and enslave the others.

Then again, the Egarlorsar's magic was no longer as strong as what it had been. Her people may have been lessened over the years, at least those who didn't live in the Broken Mountains.

"What about the Gilukkhaz?" Vyncis asked.

Tanelith blinked, looking at him in surprise. She wasn't sure what he meant.

"Ah, they've always been in their mountains, up and down the entire range," Rytha said. "It was only when they had to dig too deep into their mountains to satisfy yer people's needs that they let the wheel turn too far," she added with a nod at Tanelith.

"What do you mean?" Tanelith said.

"They didn't always have the blood metal. No, they developed that as a way of weakening the Egarlorsar, to escape from their bondage," Rytha said. "But now, crafting it, makes them a little crazy."

Tanelith blinked, confused.

"The fumes from the great furnaces," Rytha explained. "If ye listen to their songs. They tell stories of young men diving into the flames."

Vyncis nodded. "Yes, I think I remember one of those."

That got him a long look from Rytha. Tanelith wasn't about to say anything about his past to the Ilburh magician, particularly given her opinion of slavers.

Finally, Rytha gave Vyncis a crooked smile. "Ye going to be another Heobo, eh?"

Vyncis shook his head. "No, I'm not the one set for greatness. Not like Tanelith. Or my grandmother."

Rytha snorted in derision but didn't say anything.

Tanelith knew that Vyncis would speak more about it later with her.

"If yer will turn the wheel, ye got to break the Gilukkhaz of their blood metal as well. They'll complain bitterly about turning soft. But those fumes make them aggressive. They talk about the fumes of life, the fumes of war."

Tanelith nodded, feeling yet more burden land on her shoulders.

Maybe it wouldn't be her who freed her people, but her daughters.

"It's late enough, now," Rytha said abruptly. "Ye can be on your way."

She handed them more food for their packs—dried meat and

a spicy travel roll. They thanked her more than once, then made their way out of the darkened cave, into the true night beyond.

Tanelith and Vyncis shared a look when they stepped onto the flattened area just outside of the doorway. They both had so many question, so much to learn.

Hopefully, they were on the right path to get some of those answers.

CHAPTER

TWENTY-SIX

Tanelith and Vyncis traveled easily through the night, getting as far as they could without exhausting themselves. They still had a ways to go. Vyncis hoped that they'd reach the area of the stairs in the next week or so.

They were both tired of the endless traveling over the past three months. Spending the day with Rytha had been a nice respite. However, in some ways it had reminded Tanelith of how much her muscles hurt, how her soul longed for cool trees and grass. The smell of dust had soaked into her pores. She didn't know if she'd ever be able to wash herself clean of it.

Still, the nights in the desert were special. She would remember the incredible swath of stars across the open sky fondly. While she didn't care for how cold it got at night, it was still better than the ceaseless heat of the day.

That morning they camped on the edge of a dry ravine. They didn't think that the slavers were still trying to track them, at least not now. They'd probably gone back to the Ilburh lands to get more supplies and another cart, if they hadn't also perished in the sand.

Then, the slavers would be hurrying after the pair of them again. They could travel faster than Tanelith and Vyncis could:

their oxen were bred to trot for hours on end while still carrying a heavy load.

That morning they'd found a good clump of rocks that would shade them during the day. While they were setting up, Tanelith asked, "Do you think that Rytha was right? That the water drying up was why the Ilburh moved out of the desert?"

Vyncis shrugged. "That isn't the story they tell themselves. They admit to not being the first in the area, but they maintain that the god Gehor placed them on Ithlond second because he'd studied the Egarlorsar and wanted to make sure that he didn't make the same mistakes with his people."

Tanelith grimaced. She'd heard that before as well, how the Ilburh viewed themselves as a perfected people. She'd much rather believe that they'd migrated from the desert, though.

"I don't suppose we could convince them to move back to the desert," Tanelith said, still feeling sour.

Vyncis laughed. "Where do you think they'd go here?" He indicated the open area around them. "There isn't much to sell the place to anyone."

"True," Tanelith said. "Still. Maybe after the war, *if* I win the war, I can talk with Rytha about maybe resettling the old cities."

Vyncis paused before answering. He was getting much better at accessing the memories that Loba had granted him, integrating them in with his own. "One of the cities isn't that far from here, actually. We'll reach it by dawn tomorrow."

"Do we have to?" Tanelith asked.

"It's the fastest way through this area," Vyncis said. "At least as far as I can tell. Plus, Loba went this way. There's a cistern in the city that we should be able to refill our water flagons with."

"All right," Tanelith said. "Let's go see the abandoned Human cities tomorrow."

She couldn't help but shiver as she laid down. True, she'd grown up around the ruins of the great floating city of Lasirinth. But that was where her people had come from. What would an abandoned Ilburh city be like?

Though Tanelith was tired, she still didn't fall asleep immediately, unlike Vyncis who never appeared to have any problems. Tanelith hadn't said anything to him, but she felt weary unto her soul at this point. It wasn't just the travel, and the lack of rain. It was how her quest appeared to be growing.

She hadn't thought beyond stopping the slave trade. What were all of those Egarlorsar going to do, once they were no longer slaves? Where would they go? How would they live?

And what would the Ilburh do? They weren't completely dependent on slaves. Not yet. But how were they going to feed themselves if all their help left? How much food would rot in the fields if no one was there to help harvest?

On top of all that, now there were the Gilukkhaz. How was she to stop them from making the blood metal? They looked at it as a gift from the god of the mountains, Zanargil.

According to their legends, the Gilukkhaz had been enslaved by the Egarlorsar, and Zanargil was enthralled by Celionael. At that time they also lived not only under the mountain, but also farmed the valleys nearby, tithing much of their crops to the floating cities.

It was only when the great hero/priest Urur begged for Zanargil's help, and fasted in the darkest caves of the mountain for forty days, that Zanargil was finally able to heed the cries of his people.

The god of the mountain fashioned a ring out of blood metal and presented it to the Goddess Celionael, hiding the true nature of the ring. When Celionael put it on, she fell ill. That was when Urur the Liberator and the others were able to attack.

The Gilukkhaz called it The Great Reckoning. None of the Dwarves lived above the mountains, now. They instead depended on the slave trade for money, and carted in much of their food from the fields of the Ilburh.

The God Zanargil taught Urur the Liberator how to make the blood metal, who then passed it down to the rest of the priests. It was still considered a holy process.

How could Tanelith disrupt that? How could she stop the Gilukkhaz from making the blood metal? Rytha said it was poisoning them, as a people, making them crazy.

There were too many huge issues pressing down on Tanelith. And no answers, not from Celionael or the Hidden One.

Eventually Tanelith managed to fall asleep that night, only to sink into restless dreams of endless stone monoliths that she had to topple, one after another, with no end in sight.

CHAPTER

TWENTY-SEVEN

Tanelith wasn't sure what she was expecting in terms of an Ilburh city. Wide-spread houses, perhaps, like in Faburh, or even small clusters of compounds up and down what used to be a broad river.

She had *not* expected the Ilburh to build up, into the side of a cliff that overlooked the river.

The sun was just about to rise when they arrived, the air tinted pink, though no true beams had reached across the sky. The chill of the night clung to the rocks. Maybe it was colder here, because for the first time since forever, Tanelith felt as though there might be moisture in the air.

They had been traipsing along the mostly-dry bed of the river. A trickle of water still ran down the center of it.

The structure in front of her faced north, so the inhabitants would avoid the heat of the day. She counted at least twelve stories of small square windows rising up above them. It appeared to be built out of a dark red brick, with precise corners.

Had this been where the Ilburh had developed their time systems? To perfectly match the meticulousness of their building? It made a lot more sense than the towns she'd seen.

"How did people get up and down?" Tanelith said, feeling awestruck despite herself.

She didn't want to like the Ilburh, or anything they'd done. Still, she'd never seen such a place before.

"There are massive stairs inside, that lead from one level to the next," Vyncis said. "Loba had known that this place hadn't been created by the Egarlorsar, because the stairs were too short for your kind."

Tanelith couldn't help but snort. That was as good of a way of measuring a people's ruins as any, she supposed.

The trickle of water they'd been following had gone dry by the time they'd reached the city. However, the riverbed was still filled with sand and silt, not scrub. Chances were, it had been full the year before, washing away anything that had sprung up.

The rainy season would start soon, at least according to Rytha. What would it have been like, when this city was full and bustling?

Tanelith and Vyncis climbed up from the river bank to the city. In front of the open, bare doors and windows of the city appeared to have been porches at one point. The walls in front of the enclosed areas had crumbled, or been washed away by the river during a flood.

Just past the porch, Tanelith and Vyncis entered a small room. It was dark inside, even with the sun rising. Tanelith easily brought up a light for them to see by.

The room wasn't very big—maybe three people long and only two wide. Off to one side stood a doorway, and another room.

The floor was dirt, and whatever plaster had covered the walls had long ago fallen off and crumbled to dust, leaving behind faintly pink rock.

Without thinking about it, Tanelith reached out and brushed her fingers across the nearest wall.

The image didn't arrive as quickly as it would have, had this been an Elven ruin.

Tanelith suddenly had the feeling of being in a crowded place.

The people were quiet all around her, but she could still feel their presence, pushing in against her. There had been a wall in front of the opening she stood in, looking out on a gushing river. Plants dangled down from the ceiling, the Ilburh careless in how they used their life's blood.

The whole space felt cold and damp. That made Tanelith believe that the person who'd lived here had been poor, because the Ilburh loved the heat and the sun. They wouldn't voluntarily live without the sunlight, unless they couldn't afford to.

Vyncis was suddenly there, gently removing her fingertips from the wall. "What did you see?" he asked.

She told him about her vision, how crowded everything felt, how poor the people had been here. Only the rich lived up above, where it was warm and airy.

Tanelith kept having the feeling that there was something else, something more that she should be seeing.

She walked from the main room into the second room.

There, in the corner, she found what she'd been seeking. A single small brick in the corner, not bigger than her pinky on any side. It was lightweight and when she brought her light closer, she could still see letters painted on the sides.

It was a child's toy, something used to help a young one learn their letters.

There had been a child living here, with her mother. Tanelith didn't go searching deeper, to see what had happened to the little girl, if she'd been alive when her mother had left the city.

These people were gone, and very little had been left behind when they'd departed.

It felt important for her to acknowledge the little girl, though. So she stuffed the block into her bag and nodded at Vyncis, telling him to lead the way through this place to the cistern.

Then she'd have to leave. She couldn't sleep here, inside the walls of this city. There were too many memories here, pressing against her skin, and the faint feeling of the presence of all those people living here. She would spend the day outside, maybe sleeping on the porch of one of the lower rooms.

The Ilburh could never come back here, nor would she encourage them to do so. They were not a people who could live this quietly, this close together, not anymore.

But what was she going to do about them?

CHAPTER

TWENTY-EIGHT

Though Tanelith knew that Vyncis had referred to it as a cistern, she would have called it a well room.

It stank of mildew, making her sneeze. The light she shone reflected off sections of golden walls, where they weren't covered in large patches of green mold. The room was small, only a few people could comfortably fit around the wide pool of water at one time.

She would think that a water source like a well would be out in the open, available to everyone.

But she was thinking like an Egarlorsar. The Ilburh had always had people who were poor, beggars and whatnot. By making the space small, and probably guarded, they ensured that those who were rich had adequate access to water, while those who weren't, waited in long lines for their turn.

Fortunately, though the room wasn't pleasant, and held echoes of bad memories and many fights, the water coming into the pool seemed fresh. Vyncis explained that Loba had spent some time here, and had figured out that a natural spring filled the pool. It drained out naturally as well, so the water was always fresh, never stagnant.

Though it was a risk, they decided to split up for the day.

They hadn't seen anyone for ages, and they would hear any slavers long before they saw them.

The city depressed Tanelith, and she went to sleep out on the front porch of the place where they'd come in, where there had been some life and a child's laughter at one point.

Vyncis went up to the top levels to sleep for the day. The stairs were just as broad as he'd described them. Perhaps it would have been all right to sleep up there, but Tanelith wanted nothing more to do with this place, or the Ilburh, either.

She'd thought that she'd have difficulty sleeping, but found that not only did she fall asleep quickly, she didn't have any dreams.

Maybe it was the water that blessed her. She had the feeling that the well room, for all its practical purposes, had also been something of a holy place, dedicated to the goddess of rain, Kanoress.

Tanelith woke as the sun set, night creeping in on soft feet. The Ilburh city would have also gone to sleep at this time, as the Ilburh worshiped the sun. Tanelith went looking for Vyncis, going up the stairs that he'd shown her, climbing all the way to the top of the building.

The view from the top of the city was rather magnificent, she had to admit. The gorge didn't rise as far on this side, so she was able to look across the flat plain, see the sagebrush and painted rocks fade to dark lumps with the night rising. The moonlight would be magnificent from up here. As would be the sunlight—the Ilburh would have been able to see it and use it, without being burned by it.

The rooms up here were, of course, significantly larger than the ones down below. Tanelith finally felt as though she could breathe up here. The one that Vyncis had chosen still had a few murals on the walls, beautifully painted images of a faded blue sky with soft clouds floating across it, a reflection of the broad openings at the other end of the room.

"This was where Loba stayed," Vyncis said as he packed up his things. "I thought you might be interested in those." He indicated the wall that still had a mural painted on it.

Tanelith went over to look more closely at the painting. It smelled musty, of dried sand and desert. The blue was so pale, it looked as though it had just been a wash over the wall. Had it always been that color? Or at one point, had it been bright and brilliant?

Then Tanelith caught sight of what she assumed Vyncis wanted her to look at.

The clouds in the sky.

While most of the clouds were fluffy and white, there appeared to be one that was bigger and more jagged. It rose up higher than the others, more like a boat sailing across the blue.

Tanelith thought for a moment, recalling the various cities that had once floated above the world. Was this a representation of one of those? She couldn't be sure. The painting was too old, too faded.

It might be one of the cities. It also might not be.

It had never occurred to Tanelith to wonder how old the flying cities might have been. Had they always been in the sky? She had the feeling they hadn't been. There was a story about how Celionael brought her people up to the cities to fly with her.

But possibly the Ilburh of the desert had known the flying cities. Maybe even traded with them. Was that also why they had moved north? To get away from the cities, if they were accessible from the Stairs of the Gods?

Tanelith turned to look at Vyncis and merely shrugged. "I don't know," she said softly. They'd both lowered their voices while being in the desert. It called for quiet. While she felt as though when there were people living here, it had been louder, there was still a level of quiet and stillness that had been lost to the Ilburh she'd met.

Maybe being quiet was now considered old-fashioned by them. There weren't any of the Ilburh she could ask, but she would if she could.

It was finally time for them to set off again. Tanelith was glad that Vyncis had insisted that they stop here, in this abandoned place. She couldn't stop thinking about what it had been once, how the people there might have lived.

Finally, as they made their way down the empty riverbed, she asked Vyncis, "So what did you think of that city?"

Vyncis shrugged. "The Meerimec don't live that way. All on top of one another. So it seemed very alien to me, on the one hand. On the other hand, it was once a great city. Thriving. Bustling. I kept expecting to turn a corner and run into someone, you know?"

Tanelith nodded. She hadn't seen any ghosts or spirits of the dead, but she'd felt them, all around her, pressing in on her.

"Plus, whatever the Meerimec build, we build it with the intention that it will fall back to nature at some point," Vyncis continued. "It won't last for centuries, unlike these buildings."

"Why did they survive?" Tanelith asked. "Were they just built that well?"

Vyncis shook his head. "Loba went all the way to the top of the structure. There's a geometric design up there, with channels that lead to shallow bowls filled with glowing rocks. She believed that the sun powered the walls of the city, channeled through those rocks and down into the walls."

"Huh," Tanelith said. She'd never heard of such a thing before.

Then again, what had powered the flying cities? Her people might not be the only ones who had lost so much of their former glory.

She wished she could ask Olin about it. Maybe he had come across such knowledge buried in a book somewhere.

Or perhaps those in the flying city would be able to tell her.

She shouldered her pack more firmly across her back, more determined than ever to reach the stairs of the gods, to climb them, and to find one of those flying cities for herself.

TWENTY-NINE

Several nights later, Vyncis called a stop before the dawn. They were walking down a soft slope, planning on finding someplace at the bottom to rest during the day. The night have been colder than usual, and Tanelith longed for some hot tea before she slept.

"What is that?" Vyncis asked, pointing straight ahead.

Tanelith blinked her tired eyes. It looked like a light.

"Is that a house up ahead?" she asked as Vyncis turned around and started walking up the hill again.

"No," he said. "That's a village. One that Loba doesn't remember coming across."

Tanelith followed Vyncis back up the hill. They'd passed an outcropping of rock a little while before. He scurried behind it, before plopping down and resting his back against it. "The desert is huge," he complained. "And there were many parts of it that Loba didn't see. Still, she had good maps, and there weren't any towns in this part of it."

Tanelith sat down next to Vyncis. "So now we wait until sunrise? See what it is we're dealing with down there?"

He nodded grimly. "Aye," he said. He glanced over his shoulder at the rocks they were both leaning against. "This isn't the best place for hiding, but I figure it'll do, between your magic and mine."

Tanelith nodded. On the one hand, she was excited about the possibility of a town. They could get supplies!

Or was it an Ilburh town? Would the people all look at her like a slave? She couldn't image who else might have settled out here in what felt like the middle of nowhere. They hadn't come across any roads. But there must be water down there, perhaps a series of deep wells.

She closed her eyes and rested, still sitting up. She didn't want to lay down or set up camp. Not until after the sun rose and they could see what they were dealing with.

Slowly light crept back into the world. Tanelith felt it burning against her eyelids. She opened her eyes and watched the sunlight turn the plain sand and gravel at her feet golden. The air turned spicier as the smell of the sagebrush doubled. The last of the evening's chill still clung to her, but it was dissipating fast.

Tanelith turned to look at Vyncis. He appeared to be still asleep, his face relaxed and his jaw slack. He looked younger in the daylight, his curly brown hair unruly, his apple cheeks slightly reddened. He was thinner than he'd been when she'd first met him.

Then again, she was probably thinner as well. They ate what they could hunt, which wasn't much. Fortunately, Vyncis was really good at finding water for them. She was learning, slowly. It seemed to be a knack with the Meerimec, though, and not something native to the Egarlorsar.

Vyncis finally asked, "What do you see?"

Tanelith didn't blush—her skin didn't do that. She still quickly turned her gaze from her traveling companion over the rock and down at the village.

"It's a village. Maybe a hundred houses, perhaps even two hundred. Built out of red stone. Funny, square shaped buildings, with flat roofs, that I would guess are Ilburh," she said. "There's a wall around the town," she added with a growl.

The presence of a wall, particularly in what looked like an Ilburh town, meant Egarlorsar slaves.

Vyncis sighed and nodded. "Does the town look new?"

Tanelith examined the base of the wall circling the town. Rocks and dust had piled up there, blown for years by the wind. While the houses had the sharp lines and corners of the Ilburh, the edges had been blunted a little by time. The buildings themselves red or pinkish hue and the roofs were mostly white, bleached by the sunlight. They had very little slant to them, mostly they were flat.

Very little rain ever came to this area.

Just past the village she now could see what appeared to be a few fields, with cactus and some trees around the edges. However, they, too, appeared to be edged with a wall.

Her eyes drank in the sight of so much greenery, even if it was a dark color and not as varied as the woods close to her home. A range of hills blocked the eastern and southern sides of the area. Was that enough to provide water?

They were too far away to properly see any of the people of the town. The people there must be Ilburh, though. Who else would live out in so much sunshine?

A dust cloud began to accumulate in front of the gate closest to Tanelith and Vyncis. Tanelith blinked her eyes and squinted, finally making out a cart driven by oxen at the front of the large plume.

Again, they were too far away to see the people in the cart. But they had to be Gilukkhaz driving it. The cart was in their style, though they couldn't hear any slaver chains clinking off the side of it.

However, it couldn't be a Gilukkhaz town. The Dwarves no longer lived above the earth. That was an anathema to them. Vyncis had told her that even in the Ilburh towns, the slavers had dug their sleeping chambers under the earth.

Had the Gilukkhaz been visiting the town? Maybe trading, as

the back of the cart was flat, possibly filled with goods. It wasn't hooped, for people to sit there.

Stranger and stranger.

The cart immediately started heading due west, away from where Tanelith and Vyncis were hiding. There wasn't much of a road for the cart to follow. Then again, the Gilukkhaz carts didn't really need a cleared path to travel along.

She exchanged looks with Vyncis, but he didn't appear to know much more than she did.

They made a rough camp, just rolling out blankets to sleep on, huddled next to the rock which barely provided enough shade for them. It was going to be a hot day. That evening, they'd have to decide if Vyncis would go into town to see if he could buy food.

Or if Tanelith would be going, to steal some.

CHAPTER

THIRTY

Shadows had grown long by the time Tanelith awoke. Vyncis was already awake, staring at the town.

"There's something wrong there," he said without preamble.

"Wrong how?" Tanelith said.

He sighed and handed her a long tube. "Look through that," he said.

The tube was as long as her forearm. She remembered seeing something like this on Arryn's shelves. She had no idea what it was. The part Vyncis wanted her to look through was round, and maybe half as small as the other end.

"Everything's fuzzy," Tanelith complained.

Vyncis reached over and rotated the tube.

Suddenly, everything was clear. Tanelith could see the village as though she stood on top of it.

"What is this?" she asked, amazed, as she drew it away from her eye.

"It's a looking glass. It was one of Loba's gifts to me," Vyncis said. "We haven't really needed it before now, and I'd kind of forgotten that I had it."

"I see," Tanelith said frostily. Maybe he hadn't really needed it before now. But she wished she'd known about it.

It had probably been made by the Ilburh. It had that feeling to it, with long, straight lines, precisely tapered.

Still, she pressed it eagerly to her eye.

Wait.

Those weren't Ilburh that she saw. Those were Egarlorsar! And they weren't wearing any collars, at least as far as she could tell. The people were completely covered up, as well they should be, out in the sunlight as they were.

What were Elves doing out in the desert like this? Why were they here?

She didn't recognize the houses, or the layout of the village. It followed the same straight lines favored by the Ilburh.

Yet, all she saw were her people. People like the Broken Mountain people, like her, tall, fair-skinned, with dark hair and slightly pointed ears. She didn't see anyone who was shorter, or who had curly hair. She could tell that even with the hats that everyone wore, protecting themselves from the sun.

She watched for a while, a feeling of wrongness creeping over her.

The people seemed idle, for want of a better term. They were walking outside of their houses, then not doing anything but wandering aimlessly in the sun.

When they appeared to have been outside long enough, they hurried back inside, into the shade and the coolness of their houses.

"What are they doing?" Tanelith asked, confused.

"I was hoping you could tell me," Vyncis replied with a grimace. "I don't understand what I'm seeing."

"That makes two of us," Tanelith said. "You would think that they would wait until it was fully dark before they went outside."

Vyncis nodded. "We need food. Do you want to go into the town? Or should I?"

Tanelith handed the long looking glass to Vyncis then sat back, thinking. "We have enough food for a couple days, yes?"

"Yes," Vyncis replied warily.

"Can we stay here over night? See what they do?" Tanelith asked. "That way, either I'll head down before the night is over, or you'll have to go instead, tomorrow during the day."

"That makes sense," Vyncis said. He shook his head. "I don't know why, but I have a bad feeling about this."

"About the town?" Tanelith said, wanting to clarify.

"Maybe?" Vyncis said, his face squeezed together. Then he shook his head. "Loba's memories don't contain anything about a town like this. It wasn't on her maps, and she never heard anyone talking of such a place."

"I don't know," Tanelith said.

"I don't either," Vyncis said. He gave himself a good shake. "Maybe that's all that's bothering me. I don't know."

"If we should leave, move on—" Tanelith started.

"No, no. I think your plan is a good one. Spend some time here, see what they're up to," Vyncis said. "Plus, spending a night resting sounds really good right now."

"All right," Tanelith said. She had to agree that a night of rest sounded wonderful. "Let's keep watch though, through the night. See if we can figure out anything."

Vyncis nodded, eyes still staring off into the distance.

"Is there anything else you have in that bag of yours that you should tell me about?" Tanelith teased.

Vyncis threw a smile in her direction. "No, not really. Though maybe. Wait." He dug around, and out of the bottom of his pack he drew a box. It was a little longer than Tanelith's palm, and only a couple of fingers thick and deep. She vaguely remembered seeing it on one of Loba's shelves. Leaves were carved into the sides of it, floating along. The top of the small box slid out of a finely made groove.

"What is this?" Tanelith asked.

"Open it," Vyncis said.

Slowly, Tanelith slid the box open. Inside were half a dozen or so long seeds. They were each as long as her palm, and a little over a finger wide. The bottom of each seed was sharpened, like a spike, while the top was larger and tufted, similar to dandelion fluff.

Unenlightened, Tanelith looked back up at Vyncis.

"They're seeds from the guardian trees," Vyncis said. "I don't know where Loba got them. The guardian trees, well, it's said that they only fruit once every hundred years or so. I think it's more often than that, but it does generally only happen once in a person's lifetime."

"Huh," Tanelith said, handing the small box back.

"Loba insisted that I take these with me," Vyncis said as he slid the box into his pack.

"Why is that?"

Vyncis shrugged. "Don't know. Wasn't sure if she meant it as a reminder of my penance, or if she intended me to plant them someplace."

Tanelith opened her mouth, then shut it again. Surely Vyncis didn't need a reminder of his penance. He was here, after all.

"Do you want to risk a fire?" Vyncis asked after a few moments.

Tanelith shook her head. "No. The people in the town might see the light, if not the smoke. I don't think it's smart right now."

Vyncis sighed. Tanelith had to agree. If they were going to be sitting for the evening, and not moving, it was going to get pretty cold before dawn.

"The moon's waxing," Tanelith told him. "I can use it to keep warm, if you want to use my blanket."

"Thanks," Vyncis said with a grin. "I'll probably take you up on that." Then he sobered. "But one of us is going to need to go into that town in the next day or so."

Tanelith nodded. "Agreed. I just want to have a better idea what I'm walking into."

"Yes."

They were both silent for a while. Tanelith picked up the long tube, spying at people so far away.

What were they doing? Why weren't they working more? She

couldn't see the entire village from where she sat. Maybe there were other, busier parts.

But true night would be there soon. Maybe she'd be able to spy on her people better then, as there was a reason her people were called the Moon People.

THIRTY-ONE

Though Tanelith always thought of moonbeams as cool, tonight, there was also a feeling of heat. She was using her magic to keep herself warm as the temperature had plummeted with the setting of the sun. The sky was clear, and the moonlight bathed the area as completely as the sunlight usually did.

While Vyncis had stayed back with the rocks, Tanelith had moved around to the side of the village, trying to get a better idea of what the people down there were doing.

Why had they been going out into the sunlight? What had they been doing there? Now, why they were *not* going out into the moonlight? It was the first full moon after the new year. There should still be some sort of celebration.

It was only when she crept closer that she saw people going outside. But instead of being open about it, as they had been when they'd been walking in the sunlight, now, they were furtive. Sneaking out, moon-bathing for a few moments, caught up in the light, then stepping back inside.

Merchant shops lined the eastern side of the town. There was even an apothecary. The placement didn't make any sense, though. Shouldn't the merchants be along the main road? Weren't all markets in the center of a village?

The entire village was backwards. Egarlorsar outside during the day, in the bright sunlight. They even tended the fields during the day. Then not returning back outside at night, when the moon was high in the sky. The merchants on the edges of the village, and not in the center. No one even approaching the wall surrounding the village. When they'd come back from the field during the evening, they'd maintained a single-file line, as if they'd been afraid to get too close to the wall.

Tanelith returned to update Vyncis on what she'd seen. He'd been using the spyglass and didn't really have much to add. Except that all the houses had shades drawn over their windows, as if they didn't want anyone to see in.

What were they hiding? Why were they hiding? Tanelith just had more questions than answers. Vyncis couldn't help.

"I'm going to get closer to that wall," Tanelith said after a few moments.

"Are you sure that's safe?" Vyncis said. "It might have some sort of warning system built into it."

"I won't touch it," she promised. She didn't know what a wall of blood metal might do to her, even if she wasn't wearing a collar. It might be enough to drain her, however. And the night was getting on, the moon getting close setting.

"All right," Vyncis said with a grimace. "Just know that I won't have any idea how to save you."

"I'll be careful," Tanelith said. She hefted her dagger in her hand. There was something with that wall that she needed to figure out.

Tanelith gathered shadows to her, disappearing from view. Vyncis could no longer see her. Most of her own people would overlook her as well.

She picked up speed as she flowed down the hill toward the village. It felt glorious to skim across the ground this way. She hadn't used her magic like this for such a long time. She'd always felt the need to conserve it, to never spend her power foolishly while they were traveling. The only time she ever expended her magic was when she and Vyncis practiced sparing. She was getting much better at fighting, though she still had so much to learn.

Even though she was certain she was still invisible, she still slowed down considerably as she drew closer to the wall around the village.

Her mouth began to water once she smelled bread baking in a nearby house. She was momentarily confused, until she realized that it made sense to not do the baking first thing in the morning, before the heat rose, but to do it the last thing at night, and let the coolness of the evening also cool down the kitchen.

The houses closest to the wall had all their shades drawn down tight. Some of the merchants had even closed their shutters.

Why hadn't the Elves tried to make the houses prettier? She understood that they couldn't maintain any gardens. It was too hot, and they'd have to carry water to the plants. But gardens would have given them something to do, instead of lounging outside in the sunlight until they'd gotten their fill.

What were they doing inside, besides baking? She listened, but she couldn't hear laughter or singing. Not even prayers.

She didn't know what was wrong with these people, but she suspected they weren't normal Egarlorsar, no matter how much they might look like her.

Tanelith shifted her focus from the houses to the wall that separated her from the village. It came up a little past her waist, so it was easy to see over. She didn't get the sense of anything magical emanating from it.

Then again, she'd probably have to touch it, as that appeared to be how most magic was invoked.

The wall was made out of baked bricks. The perfect curve of the wall surprised her. Such curvature was an Egarlorsar trait, not something from the Ilburh, unlike the ugly houses.

Blown sand piled up around the base of the wall. Dust covered the top of it. Tanelith shivered remembering the wall in

Faburh, which had broken shards of glass sticking out of the top of it.

Tanelith had practiced transforming the dagger in the moonlight while keeping herself hidden in shadows. It had taken a lot of effort, but Vyncis finally could no longer see her when she made the change.

Would her own people be able to find her if she used her magic? She didn't know. Then again, all the windows were closed and barred.

Tanelith took a chance and slid some of the cool moonlight into the blade, extending it to its intermediate form. She paid attention to how it felt when she brought it closer to the wall.

However, the blade didn't react in the slightest. It didn't notice anything to fear in the wall itself.

Then again, the blade couldn't recognize blood metal either.

Slowly, Tanelith reached out with the knife, ready to whirl away at the slightest noise.

Finally, she touched the tip of the dagger to the wall.

Nothing happened.

She didn't feel any ill magic. Didn't hear any gong or bell sound, alerting the village to her presence.

Nothing.

Tanelith shifted the blade back to its ceremonial form. It went without hesitation. Clearly, it didn't feel threatened by anything, either the wall or the village.

With great daring, Tanelith made herself reach out and brush her fingers across the cool bricks.

All she felt was the smooth surface of the brick, followed by the grainy texture of the mortar.

Not even a hint of blood metal had been woven into the wall.

Frustrated, Tanelith stepped closer. She stared at the wall, but it appeared to be just that. A wall.

Finally, Tanelith reached out and rested her palm against the brick. It was still much smoother than she'd thought it would be, the mortar a rough contrast. She breathed in, and smelled the heat of the desert still locked inside.

But the wall gave her nothing. Not even a hint of what it was. That was strange. Normally, she could get the sense of a building by touching it, could discern the use of a wall in a ruin.

This wall held onto nothing.

Tanelith took a step back. Was it because the wall was so new? That was the only thing she could think of that would feel this way. Even the rocks in the desert gave her more of an impression, of them waiting patiently as the sun baked them, the night froze them.

After pausing for another moment, Tanelith sidled away, heading toward one of the gates. The circular wall had four of them, one in each of the cardinal points. (Another Ilburh thing.)

However, the wall maintained its nondescript characteristics. It wasn't antagonistic to her, or to anyone, really. It was a cipher, unbroken.

Or it was not magical in the least, despite how the town's people treated it.

Frustrated, Tanelith headed back to where Vyncis was waiting. He appeared to be asleep, his mouth open and his head sagging to one side.

Why was he asleep like that? Why hadn't he laid down? Had he actually fallen asleep while sitting up? That wasn't like him. He'd said he'd keep watch.

Tanelith crept over to him.

A sour smell of sickness rose up to her.

"Vyncis?" she said softly, shaking his shoulder. "Wake up."

Had he fallen ill?

His bleary eyes blinked at her. "Snake…" he whispered. Then he toppled to the side, no longer able to hold himself up.

Tanelith saw the bite on his hand, where fangs had sunk deep.

Vyncis had always been afraid of snakes. And he'd had a bad feeling about this place, though neither Tanelith or Vyncis had been able to figure out what the problem was.

Tanelith listened to his labored breathing.
He'd been poisoned.
She had no magic to help him.
And he was going to die if she couldn't save him.

CHAPTER

THIRTY-TWO

Tanelith debated for a moment. Should she go and fetch someone from the town to come and help? Or should she take Vyncis down there?

While she couldn't necessarily lift him up on her own, using her magic she certainly could. The moon had been near to full that evening, so she wouldn't use up all her strength.

She left their packs where they were, then picked up Vyncis. He seemed frail in her arms. His heart was racing. He smelled like bile.

Just as she got sick using Meerimec magic and tree stepping, she knew that traveling, wrapped in moonlight and shadows, would weaken Vyncis.

She didn't have time or the strength to just carry him, though.

Tanelith raced back to the village, hugging Vyncis close. It was a bit awkward with the dagger in her one hand. However, she wasn't about to let that go, either.

A faint tingle went through Tanelith when she crossed through the gate to the town. She couldn't do anything about that, though. She didn't have any time to figure out what sort of magic she'd just invoked.

She'd slice up the wall with her sword if it tried to contain her.

Tanelith raced around to the eastern side of the village, to the apothecary shop she'd seen.

It surprised her that the door was unlocked.

She slipped in quickly, shutting the door behind her.

An old man stood behind the counter, lit by a glowing candle in a holder standing beside him. He blinked at her, as if waking from a dream. He wore a long, informal robe, done in shades of white and cream, that went from his neck down to the floor, as well as long sleeves that opened with wide cuffs at the wrists. Silver hair fell to his shoulders instead of carrying down past his chest, the points of his ears sticking up on the sides. His bulbous nose jutted out from a flat face, below watery gray eyes. No whiskers covered his chin.

He seemed very old to her, and worn out, despite the lack of wrinkles on his smooth skin.

The front of the shop was very small, much smaller than Old Odin's place. Only a few people could fit on her side of the counter. Behind the counter, colorful jars filled with mystical herbs filled the shelves. The shop smelled of medicinal tea. It was cooler than Tanelith had expected, as if the heat of the day had never warmed the place.

Tanelith stripped off the last of the shadows so the old man could see that she carried someone.

"Oh. My," was all he said. He froze for a moment, before beckoning her to follow him, back behind the counter, into a room behind the front of the shop.

With an impatient wave of his hand, lights flared on the walls.

Tanelith blinked, taken back by the sudden bright light.

"Put him here," the old man said, indicating a long table standing in the middle of the room.

Tanelith did and stepped back. She took a look around the room.

Cool crystals stuck in bronze sconces lit the room. At least that was something she was familiar with. However, the walls were starkly white. It struck her as odd, because that wasn't necessarily a color that the Egarlorsar used. Wooden cabinets, also white, covered at least half the space. There were no windows, which was also strange. Didn't all healers need the moon to help them in their work?

The old man examined Vyncis' hand, tutting and muttering under his breath. "When did this happen?" he asked, his voice gentle despite the urgency of his words.

"A short while ago," Tanelith said.

He looked sharply at her for a moment before he gave her a smile, nodding his head. "You aren't from around here," he stated. "I am Amindur. I think you brought your friend here in time."

Amindur pulled open a drawer from the cabinet behind him, removing instruments from it. "You may have to hold your friend down while I drain the poison," he said.

Tanelith nodded. She hung the dagger from her belt and reached out, holding onto Vyncis' shoulders as directed by Amindur.

The old man held a short blade in his hand. It was no longer than her thumb, though twice as wide. "I need to open the wound," he explained.

He didn't wait until Tanelith had acknowledged or even processed the words. He sliced the skin on Vyncis' hand between the two fang points, then made a second slice across it, like an X.

Vyncis startled at the pain, though his eyes didn't open again. Tanelith tightened her fingers around his shoulders, holding him firmly to the table.

Tanelith only caught a word here and there that Amindur started chanting. It gave her relief when she heard him call on the Goddess Celionael to help.

The blood flowed cleanly from the wound, pouring out across the clean cotton rag that Amindur had pulled from the drawer. Then he picked up what looked like a tapered willow branch, only about as wide as her pinky, though at least as long as her forearm. Golden thread was wrapped around the smooth wood in a crisscrossing pattern.

Amindur lightly tapped Vyncis' arm with the willow branch, starting close to where the wound now merely dripped, then continued tapping, going up his forearm.

As he continued, the wood under the golden threads started to darken. By the time it reached Vyncis' shoulder, it had gone from a light, almost white wood to a deep purple color.

However, Amindur merely nodded when he saw it. He sang a snatch of a hymn that Tanelith recognized, asking the Goddess for clear vision. Then he took a different piece of wood and started scraping down Vyncis' arm with it.

The scraper was rectangular, about the length and width of her palm, made out of a thin wood. It kept its color as the old man worked, staying a rosy red hue.

The blood coming out of Vyncis' hand changed. Instead of red and thin, it was now thick and darkened, more like dried blood, dribbling out of the wound.

Vyncis started to breathe harder, as if he was racing. His heart pounded under Tanelith's palms, where she held him down on the table. The smell of bile and sour sickness filled the small room. Tanelith had to look away in order to take a deep breath.

However, she wouldn't allow herself to let go of her friend. Particularly not when he started bucking.

"Hold him," Amindur commanded, still using that almost whispered tone.

Tanelith used all her strength and weight to keep Vyncis down on the table, though he was trying to thrash from side to side now.

"Shh, it's all right," Tanelith told Vyncis softly. "We're helping you. Removing the poison. You'll be fine. Shh."

Amindur smiled and nodded, though his attention never

wavered from the work he was doing on Vyncis' arm, scraping the poison down Vyncis' arm and out of his body.

By the time Amindur reached the wound with the wooden scraper, Vyncis had settled down. His rasping breath was the only sound in the small room.

Amindur used the willow wand again, tapping up Vyncis' arm. This time, he barely reached the Meermec's elbow before it turned purple.

"Good," Amindur said as he started scraping again.

Vyncis started struggling as soon as the rectangle of wood touched his skin. Tanelith held on tightly, wondering if it was always like this, or if this was some sort of reaction Vyncis was having because he was a Meerimec.

By the third time Amindur used the willow wand to test, most of the poison appeared to have been forced from Vyncis' body. Just a bit remained close to the wound. Still, Amindur calmly pushed at it, trying to get as much as he could.

Tanelith found herself starting to breathe when she realized that the sour smell of bile and sickness had dissipated.

Amindur cleaned up Vyncis' hand and bandaged it. "It will take a few days for him to regain his strength," he said, looking up at Tanelith again. "Then, you can travel on again. You cannot stay here, though. You'll have to find shelter somewhere outside of town."

"We will," Tanelith said, not sure why they couldn't stay. "Thank you," she added. "I don't know how to repay you."

"Tell me your tales, until the sun rises," he said simply. "Where you are coming from, where you are going. I'm assuming the Stairs, yes?"

"Yes," Tanelith said, relieved. "I will gladly tell you my tales. But what is this place? Why are you here? Why do you go out into the bright sunlight?"

Amindur gave her a mirthless smile. "That's too long of a tale, I'm afraid. Much longer than the night we have. None of us want to be here. We are all held here, by our blood."

"By your blood?" Tanelith said, surprised. "What do you mean?"

"Have you ever heard of something called blood metal?" Amindur asked. "Or know of how it's used?"

Tanelith stiffened, then showed him first one side of her neck, then the other, where her scars were still evident. "I was a collared slave," she said.

Amindur looked at her, his eyes wide, astonished. Then he peered more carefully at her, as if examining a great prize. "I am changing my fee," he said. "I want some of your blood. To see if I can use it to perhaps come up with a cure to free us."

"Gladly," Tanelith said. "How are you held here?" she asked as Amindur scurried around the room, collecting tiny glass straws and larger vials, stoppered with corks.

"The reason the blood metal is so effective against the Egarlorsar is because it is made from our blood," Amindur said.

Tanelith gasped. She'd had no idea.

"Oh, don't worry," Amindur said, patting her hand. He paused, looking down at the handpiece she was wearing, then he went back to his preparations. "While your blood would work to make the metal, it's easier if the blood is already contaminated. Like ours is, here."

"Who contaminated your blood? How?" Tanelith asked.

Amindur picked up the fat blade again, cleaning it thoroughly as he talked. "The Gilukkhaz," he said. "In a terrible magic ritual. We were all captured, meant to become slaves, I believe. But they brought us here, instead."

"Can't you escape?" Tanelith asked. Surely these people would be able to find the watering holes that Vyncis had led her to.

"We can't get past the wall, not with our tainted blood," Amindur said. "There's a second wall, out around the fields, so we can't go that way either. And even if we could, our very nature has been disturbed. Moonlight no longer fulfills us. Instead, we require sunlight. It's a very tiring, strange existence."

The old man paused. Tanelith could see the exhaustion that lurked behind his eyes. "If we kill ourselves, they just bring in a new person, someone who they've recently kidnapped. If we hang on, we are saving others from this fate. Some can't always hold on, though."

The bleakness in his soft voice struck Tanelith's soul. It was a cursed existence.

"The Gilukkhaz come every few days to collect our blood, count heads, bring supplies. We have everything we need here. Except, of course, our families, our friends, our homes." He shook his head and reached for the hand that wore the handpiece. "Should I use this hand for drawing out some of your blood?"

"No," Tanelith said, sliding him the hand that didn't have the handpiece. "Where do they make the blood metal?" She would have thought that all the furnaces would be closer to the mountains.

"They've set up a new refinery close to here, to meet the demand for it, when they discovered hills nearby to contain the right sort of ore," Amindur admitted. "This town is only a few years old."

"Built by the Ilburh?" she asked.

Amindur nodded. "This is going to hurt," he warned just before he made a small cut in her skin, two fingers up from her wrist.

Tanelith gasped but stayed still.

Interestingly, the handpiece abruptly transformed, growing spikes, even though the dagger remained at her waist.

Amindur kept his movements very steady and sure, picking up one of the tiny glass straws and sipping away her blood. "I see," he said, nodding his head toward the handpiece.

Tanelith held up her hand, trickling a slight bit more power into the handpiece, transforming it into the full milky-white glass armor gauntlet, then releasing it completely so that the handpiece returned to its normal, decorative shape.

She told Amindur of her family, of being kidnapped, of her

escape. She told him of the Broken Mountains, and how if they could escape, they would be welcome there. She was determined that the people of the Broken Mountain keep their word.

They wouldn't reject the people from this town based on their looks, that was for certain.

"There have only been a few who have passed through here, carrying news from the outside world," Amindur said as Tanelith finished. "Maybe one or two a year, for the four years that I've been here. All of them believed that there was something at the Stairs."

Tanelith nodded. "Did they all believe that there were still cities of the gods, flying among the clouds?"

"Aye," Amindur said. "Though I've never seen such a thing."

"I have," Tanelith told him.

He gave her a sweet smile. "The gods themselves would be interested in one such as yourself, who bears the armor you do." He glanced at Vyncis, who still slept soundly. "You are lucky to have a guide. Many of those I saw were sick, or on the verge of dying. You two, though, are still strong."

"Yes," Tanelith said. "I would have died several times before now, if not for Vyncis."

Amindur bandaged up her arm as neatly as he had Vyncis. He stashed all her blood away in his cabinets, then sniffed the air.

"The dawn is almost here. You need to be gone," he said seriously. "The others in the town—they won't take as kindly to you as I have. They will see you as a threat. If you're here, they will wonder if maybe one of them will be killed by the Gilukkhaz when they return."

Tanelith nodded. "Thank you," she said. "May you find a way out of here quickly."

"Thank you," he said in return. "And may you find what you're truly seeking."

Tanelith thought about Amindur's words as she flowed out of the town, carrying Vyncis again. She'd asked for the name of the town, but no one could agree on a name.

Except merely calling it "Cursed."

There would be other cursed towns, probably closer to the mountains, where other Egarlorsar would be kept for their blood.

She was going to have to free them too.

CHAPTER

THIRTY-THREE

It took three days for Vyncis to regain his strength. Amindur had sent along a tea that he wanted Tanelith to prepare for him, to help Vyncis rid himself of any remaining poison.

It smelled as vile as it tasted, but Vyncis choked it down every morning and evening. Mostly, he slept and Tanelith kept watch.

She went back down to visit Amindur every night, gathering supplies and telling more tales.

If Tanelith was a great leader, maybe she'd follow the Gilukkhaz cart back from the town to the refinery. Maybe even destroy the metal works, shut down the mine there. She couldn't do that, though. She had no idea what would happen to the people in the cursed town. Would the Gilukkhaz just move them to a different town? Or would they let them die?

Until Amindur found a cure for his people, she couldn't destroy the metal works, no matter how tempting that might be.

It was surprisingly difficult to say goodbye to Amindur the last night. She'd grown fond of the old Elf, of his gentle ways. She added his name to the list of names of all the women on the carts, a litany she recited to herself now and again, reminding herself why she was making this journey, the people who needed saving.

Though she couldn't save them all, she was still going to try.

When Vyncis was finally strong enough, they flowed away from the cursed town, heading directly east now, toward the stairs. They traveled easily for the first few days, never pushing too hard, as Vyncis would still tire early after they'd traveled for a night.

Tanelith found herself breathing easier one evening as they flowed across the empty spaces between mountainous foothills. It wasn't until morning and the dawn creeping across the sky that she realized the air was softer, finally. While it was still warm, it wasn't going to get nearly as hot that day.

Trees, actual trees, had gathered at the foot of the large hill in front of them. They weren't as tall as the pines near her home, nor as colorful as the maples or elms. However, despite how stunted they looked, they had leaves growing. Loba called them scrub oak, according to Vyncis.

Tanelith could tell that Vyncis was heading straight for the nearest grove. It wouldn't give them as much protection as possibly an outcrop of rock. She didn't tease him about it, though. She, too, had missed the greenery.

The ground under the half-dozen trees of the grove was pitted and rocky. Dried grass clung to the rocks, swaying in the early morning breeze. It still smelled of the desert, of sun-baked stone and desert sage. The leaves looked like small oak leaves. Instead of growing up and tall, the trees grew more to the sides.

Tanelith couldn't quite reach the top of the trees while standing, but it was close.

She grinned at Vyncis, who hung his head for a moment before he grinned back at her. Then, he appeared to give in, and leaned forward, embracing the tree in a fierce hug.

"Trees," he murmured.

Tanelith nodded. She suspected that she was going to have the same reaction when she finally stood outside in the rain again.

They quickly set up camp, weaving nests into the branches of the trees. They weren't out of sight, not really. Not unless they used their magic to hide themselves.

Despite the heat, and how little the leaves protected her from the sunlight that day, she still slept better than she had in a long while.

When the night came, Tanelith and Vyncis decided to spend an extra day there. They'd found a small stream close by, and had filled their meager supply of water. In addition to catching some fish, they'd trapped a couple of rabbits. Young spring onions were just starting to bloom, along with dandelions.

"The land changes from here on," Vyncis told Tanelith after they'd finished their meal. The rabbit was still smoking, so they'd have more dried meat. "We'll go around the larger hills more often than climbing up or down them."

Tanelith nodded. "It's strange that there aren't any people here," she said, "in this softer land."

Vyncis shrugged. "It's still a hard existence down here. Not much water. Lots of game, if you're patient. But it would be difficult to grow crops here."

"Are there tiny villages in the area? Tucked away?" Tanelith asked. The land here was beautiful, despite how empty it felt to her.

"There are," Vyncis said. "Mainly Ilburh," he added after a few moments, obviously consulting his memories. "They're really isolated and don't welcome travelers. Loba had a couple of bad run-ins with them, then avoided anyplace inhabited after that."

Tanelith wondered whether her people would want to settle here, once they'd been freed. It would be a very different existence than what they'd been living before. Still, she could see a few coming this way. Particularly as open as the land felt, how well the moon shone down, bathing everything.

She knew that being in such open spaces soothed her soul, particularly after being so closed in, when she'd been in Faburh. Or perhaps the people from the cursed towns would settle here. Find some way to grow what they needed, trapping the rest.

The mountains spoke to her, the tall peaks singing their praises to the Goddess. As spring crept into the land, her heart soared, delighting in the brilliant blue, white, pink, and yellow flowers. While many of the pine trees kept the dark green of fall and winter, their ends had turned the brightest green and were soft to the touch. The smell of pine finally overwhelmed the scents from the desert.

Tanelith and Vyncis sparred that night. She put on her full armor, filling it with moonlight. The dark of the moon had just passed them and Tanelith was finding it easier to support the armor again.

Even wearing the full suit, Vyncis still found ways to grapple her to the ground. She was much better at evading his strikes, particularly as they still went slowly at the start.

At speed, she frequently moved the wrong direction, or used the wrong arm to try to deflect a blow.

Part of it she knew was because both she and the suit were used to working with the sword. So when a blow came, even if it would be better blocked by her left forearm, she still turned into it with her right.

So they practiced. At least the dirt shed quickly from the milky-white armor when Vyncis tackled her to the ground.

She had a feeling that most of the guard who wore such armor had never had such a humiliating experience.

However, Tanelith was determined to learn how to fight.

"You're better than you were," Vyncis assured her as he gave her a hand to help her up.

"Thanks, I think," Tanelith said sourly. "But when am I going to get good?"

"You didn't grow up wrestling and fighting like I did," Vyncis said. "It's going to take years before you achieve a lot of skill. However, you have an advantage. That suit is helping you, teaching you how to move. I think if you listened to it more, you might get better quicker."

"But then that's the suit learning, not me," Tanelith complained. She didn't quite know how to explain it, but she tried. "Sure, when I let the suit defend me, I do much better. What happens the first time I'm in a fight and I don't have the suit on? I won't know how to do anything."

"So we keep practicing," Vyncis assured her. "Though, if you're leading an army, I'm not sure how much fighting you'll actually be doing, versus directing your warriors."

Tanelith sighed. "And how am I supposed to learn how to do that? How to lead and direct an army?"

Vyncis gave her a wry grin. "I figure you'll have to learn by doing." Then he sobered. "Remember, no one has large armies of warriors. No one is familiar with battle, not like that. Everyone is going to be confused and mess up at the start. You'll just have to figure it all out faster than everyone else."

Tanelith considered his words as she dozed that day in dappled sunlight, shaded by the leaves of the tree she rested in.

She was going to have to get good advisors when it came time to battle. Old Orin came to mind. There must be accounts of battles in his books. Maybe he would be able to teach her what she needed to do.

But who else? Would the elders of the Broken Mountains know anything? Would they turn away from selling their own people into slavery, or would they fight her from their desire to remain "pure?"

How about the elders of her people, along the Dorwine river? Would they help? Did they have any great knowledge among them? Or were they already making deals with the slavers? Were there even now Dwarves plying their trade up and down the Dorwine?

It still felt as though there were too many daunting tasks in front of her.

If there was at least one city still floating, surely they would have people who could help her.

She'd just have to convince them to come out of the clouds and set foot on the soil again.

Hopefully, that would be an easier task than managing an army.

She fell asleep eventually, dreaming restless dreams of shouting warnings that no one heard.

CHAPTER

THIRTY-FOUR

Tanelith had thought a lot about what a rock formation that represented stairs looked like.

However, in all her imaginings, she'd never imaged something like what she was seeing.

The dawn had just arrived, but they were going to walk a few hours in the light, until they reached the valley below. It appeared flattish, with familiar sage covered most of it, though a few stubborn trees held on here and there.

Sprouting from the ground were rock formations unlike any she'd ever seen.

Some of them looked like mushrooms, with fat bulbous heads and skinnier bodies. Others looked like asymmetric arches formed out of rock that had been sculpted by the wind. Still others had the appearance of blocks that had been stacked, one on top of another, by a hasty toddler.

The reds, yellows, and tans seemed vibrant under the dome of blue sky, as if a recent rain had washed away all the dust. They'd startled a herd of small deer—much more petite than the animals she was used to around her home—who had scampered between the rocks, dodging around them like water running across a stony bank. Birds nested at the tops of more than one of the structures, scolding them as they approached. Tanelith could smell the water nearby, and was delighted by the sight of a small creek making its way across the plain.

"What is this place?" she asked Vyncis as she followed behind him, swerving around the first of the rock structures. Once they reached the base of the valley, it surprised her how tall these structures were. She'd assumed that she'd be as tall as they were. Instead, they were all three or four men tall.

Vyncis gave her a crooked grin. "Loba called it the Valley of the Statues. Kind of looks like that, doesn't it?"

Tanelith nodded. "What made these?" Were these statues that the gods had placed in this valley for some reason?

Vyncis thought for a moment. "There's an old myth that Loba dug up, about a town that refused to go back under the mountain when the God Zanargil ordered all the Gilukkhaz to return there. He was supposed to save them from some great flood."

Tanelith had heard stories of the great flood from her people as well. It was one of the reasons why the Goddess Celionael had created the floating cities, to support her people above the earth when it was flooded.

"These people refused. So Zanargil turned them into statues, and placed them here, far from the mountains, so they could forever mourn their choice."

Tanelith couldn't help her shiver. The Goddess Celionael would certainly punish people if they wouldn't obey her, but her punishments weren't cruel, not like this.

"That's awful," she said after a few moments.

Vyncis shrugged. "We'll camp just up here, next to the creek, for the day. Tomorrow, we'll climb out of this valley, around that hill, and then…"

"And then?" Tanelith prompted.

Vyncis blew out a deep breath. "I think, and then we'll start seeing the formations that form the stairs."

"That's good, right?" Tanelith asked, peering at Vyncis.

"It is," he said slowly. "But what will we do when we get there?"

Tanelith blinked at him, surprised by the question. "We climb," she said simply.

"I'm not sure that's the right response," he said. "You'll see when we get there. I'm not sure that even with our magic, we'll be able to make it up the side of that slope."

Tanelith shrugged. She didn't know, and wouldn't until they'd seen the place. "How many days?" she asked.

"Two, maybe three," Vyncis said. He nodded at her with a sad smile. "Then you'll be on your way, and I can go back to Gishem Woods."

"Wait, aren't you coming with me?" she said, shocked.

"I've thought about it a lot as we've traveled here," Vyncis said. "I'm not sure I want to."

"You don't want to see the cities of the gods?" Tanelith said, puzzled.

"I have done my penance," Vyncis said. He gave her a lopsided grin. "I have helped you succeed. Brought you to the place that you needed to go. And learned that yes, the Gilukkhaz and the Ilburh are wrong to enslave the Egarlorsar. I see that, I see that I was wrong to think that you were lesser than any of the other races, Tanelith."

Tanelith nodded. She remembered back at the beginning, when Vyncis wouldn't use her name, when he sometimes wouldn't meet her eye. It had taken a while for him to come to rely on her, for him to trust her to watch over him and keep guard.

Just as it had taken some time for her to believe that he wouldn't betray her in a heartbeat, given the chance.

"I think that Loba will allow me back in, now," he said, nodding. "It might be why she chose to be buried with the guardian trees, you know. Just to make sure I did the right thing."

Tanelith didn't reply. She thought Vyncis might be right. However, she also believed that Loba had seen the coming war, and had wanted to make sure that her people were safe, and could stay safe in their woods.

"Let's set up camp here," Vyncis said, indicating a flat area next to one of the mushroom-type of rock structures, close to the water. "I want to see if I can entice one of those deer in to come back."

"All right," Tanelith said, knowing that if their hunt was successful, they'd be there for an extra day, processing the meat. While she was impatient to get to their destination, she also understood the delay.

If Tanelith was going off on her own in a few days, it made sense for Vyncis to have extra food. Processing an entire animal by one's self was a lot of work.

They set up camp. Tanelith already had nostalgia setting in.

Just a few more days, then everything would be different.

Or so she hoped.

CHAPTER

THIRTY-FIVE

After successfully butchering and smoking the meat from the deer, Tanelith and Vyncis made their way out of the Valley of the Statues and around the next rise of hills.

Tanelith had been expecting more of the same, flat ground with rising hills. Instead, all of the ground had turned rocky and hilly. More trees grew in this area—real trees, tall with large leaves—and the air was blessedly cooler during the day, when they slept. Birds regularly sang from the branches, and in addition to the snakes and lizards, she saw mice and smaller rodents again, including rabbits. The air smelled of pine instead of sage, a scent she'd missed so much.

The structure of the stairs was impossible to miss. It rose high above the trees, a spire of red rock. The top of it looked thin, as though possibly she could wrap her arms around it.

The "steps" of the structure would be impossible for a person to climb. Each vertical slope was at least a person's height between broken off, flattish ledges. As they drew closer, Tanelith realize that only a giant could walk up the supposed stairs.

She suddenly saw what Vyncis had been talking about, how difficult it would be to actually climb the side of the structure.

Tanelith refused to give up hope. Both Rytha and Amidror had heard of other people coming here. If it was impossible to reach the floating cities from the stairs, surely they would have returned and said so?

Unless they'd died on their return journey…

It was so much easier traveling through this part of the world than it had been traveling through the desert areas. They even talked about switching their schedule, to travel through the day instead of the night. However, if Vyncis was going to turn right around and leave, it didn't make sense for him to change once, then change back.

Tanelith knew that her people would love this area. There were enough trees for them to use for building, and the creeks here ran clear and fresh. She was fairly certain that even in the middle of summer there would be enough water.

Had there been a great flood through this area at one point? Was that why her people had moved to the north? She had no idea, and no way of determining such a thing. It was one more thing, on her overly long list of items, to ask Old Olin to look up at some point.

If she wasn't in the middle of a war and needed his attention elsewhere.

They traveled at their usual pace, neither speeding up or slowing down as they made their way to the base of the stairs. Tanelith was happy about that, though she sometimes wanted to travel both faster to get there, as well as slower to spend more time with Vyncis.

They needed no map, and didn't have to rely on Loba's memories at this point. The stairs were obvious. All they had to do was to get clear enough of the trees to look up and see it there in front of them.

After a few days, they finally broke through the trees and underbrush and arrived at the base of the stairs themselves late in the evening, just before dawn.

The structure was huge, much bigger than Tanelith had believed when staring at it from across the valley. It would take her a while to walk all the way around the base, perhaps as much as an Ilburh hour.

Sandy, red ground surrounded the area, the trees all hanging back, as if they'd been banished from the rock. On the sides facing the stairs, all the vegetation looked stunted, as if it had been burned and never recovered.

Tanelith felt oddly exposed walking the short distance from the edge of the trees to the red rocks.

"Did you see this?" Vyncis called from one side.

Tanelith turned and walked back to where he stood, still under the trees on one side.

It was the remains of someone's camp. It had been a long while since they'd been there, perhaps as much as a year. There was a pack stashed beneath a piles of rocks. Whatever food had been left in the pack had been found and eaten by rodents, who'd also torn apart the cloak that had been stuffed in there, using it for their nests.

From what remained of the leather pack, Tanelith guessed that it had been an Elf who had camped there. The pack had smooth stitching and elegant lines, similar to the bag she herself carried, that had been given to her by the people in the Broken Mountains.

"Where do you suppose they went?" Tanelith said.

Vyncis snorted at her. "Up, don't you think? They went up the stairs into the cities of the gods and never returned?"

Tanelith shivered. She'd had to believe this entire time that she was right, that Loba was correct in her assessment of the stairs.

This pack just confirmed that possibly, *maybe*, it hadn't all been a wild dream that she'd been chasing the entire time.

"We should camp here," Tanelith said. "Then, tonight, after sunset, I'll see if I can find a path up."

She turned back to the stairs formation and looked up. The

top of the stairs remained hidden from sight, and clouds gathered on the horizon.

She didn't know how she was going to get up there. But if others had done it, she could as well.

Or die trying.

THIRTY-SIX

Tanelith found it almost impossible to rest and sleep that day. She dozed a little. But she kept waking up with a sense of rising excitement and anxiety.

She was *here*. Now, she just had to figure out how to get up *there*.

She examined the red rock for foothold and handholds and generally came up lacking. There was no obvious path up the sheer face. Maybe there was a more obvious track on the other side of the rock structure, though she doubted it.

It was another puzzle for her to figure out.

As the afternoon drew long shadows from the trees, Tanelith stirred from the nest she'd been resting in, climbing down and stalking toward the base.

The heat held by the stones and red earth surrounding the stairs was formidable. She could see it contorting the air, creating waves.

Had this clearing been made deliberately? Was this why the trees had never snuck in closer?

And if this was what this portion of the formation was like, how hot would the actual structure be?

After Tanelith had crossed the gap between the trees and the rocks, the temperature dropped. It was just the perfect ring of stones around the stairs that was so hot.

It wasn't natural, that much she was certain of. Someone had made that ring, to gather in the heat of the sun.

Wasn't that an Ilburh thing? To use the heat of the day? It wasn't something her people would naturally do.

Tanelith stopped on the inside circle and turned back to the outer, overly warm ring. She bent down and touched the hot stones.

Vyncis had said that the top of the city they'd stayed in had geometric designs carved into it, along with bowls filled with stones that remained hot. That somehow, the power of the sun was diverted into the walls of the city below, to keep them strong.

Was this perfect circle of hot stones doing the same? What was it powering?

Tanelith took the time in the fading sunlight to walk all the way around the rock structure, looking for a way up. It took her less time than she'd initially estimated, maybe only half of an Ilburh hour.

All she saw was blank, faceless red rock. There were no obvious footholds. On the far side, she saw where someone had carted other stones in, trying to build a path going up. They hadn't gotten very far, though, just a few rocks that Tanelith walked up carefully, searching for a handhold.

She found nothing.

Disheartened, she returned to where Vyncis was still resting. Only he'd gotten up as well, and was tending their cooking fire.

Possibly, this would be the last time they'd eat together.

Tanelith shook her head against the tears that threatened. She would miss Vyncis, his wry laughter, his quiet, gentle guidance.

Would she even see him again after this?

Of course she would. She would make a point of it.

That settled, she walked over and they fell quickly into their usual routine. He'd tend the fire and she'd fill their water jugs, get herself packed and ready to go for the night.

Only tonight, he wouldn't be coming with her.

Tanelith told Vyncis about the heated rocks, and her speculation that perhaps they fueled...something.

He cocked his head to the side as he thought, carefully stirring the venison stew they would have as their last meal.

"Take another look at the stairs," he said after a few moments. "Tell me what you see. Or rather, what you *don't* see."

Puzzled, Tanelith turned to examine the rock formation again. They were sitting just under the trees, so she couldn't see all of it.

It was just bare rock with sheer sides, rising up impossibly high. The "steps" didn't start for two or three stories up, if this were a house. The flat areas were clear of weeds and brush. Then the rock climbed again. Would there be any handholds up there? If she could only get high enough to see!

Her gaze returned to the flat area, notched into the side of the stairs. There was something there...

No, Vyncis was right. There was something *missing*.

"Why doesn't grass grow on any of the flat areas?" Tanelith asked. "Or any bushes? Something should be growing there."

Vyncis nodded. "Aye. I saw that, and it bothered me. I'm wondering if the stairs also get hot, too hot for things to grow there."

Tanelith nodded. "But why? Why would it get so warm there?"

"I don't know," Vyncis admitted. "I do wonder if more of the red rock, like what is around the base, are also scattered up there, on the flat parts."

"If you had a flying city, I suppose you could drop rocks off on flat surfaces," Tanelith said slowly. She herself couldn't fly. She also didn't recall any myths of heroes or gods flying either.

Not in anything but one of the cities.

"Again, coming back to the why of it," Tanelith said after a few moments. "Is it powering something? Like that Ilburh city?"

Vyncis shrugged. "Hopefully after tonight, you'll find someone you can ask."

"Yes," Tanelith said. Then she deliberately turned her back to the rock formation. "The night will come soon enough. In the meantime, I need to thank you again for helping me get here."

"You're welcome," Vyncis said. "I can't say that I was initially happy with the penance that Gran gave me. But it didn't turn out too badly."

"Didn't you always want to travel, though? Like Loba, or even Adas?"

"Aye, I did," Vyncis said. "But to travel on my own, not because I had to guide someone. I didn't want to be running from slavers. I would have liked to stay places longer, instead of the constant need to keep moving."

Tanelith nodded. While they hadn't rushed on their way, they hadn't dallied either. She knew that Vyncis had wanted to spend more time exploring the old Ilburh city they'd spent only a single night in. Possibly other places as well.

"You can travel more slowly on the way back," Tanelith assured him. "Take your time to explore."

"I might do that," Vyncis said. "Though honestly, I have such a longing for the trees of my home."

"I understand," Tanelith said. She felt the same. When would she return to her home village? How could she get word to her parents that she was still alive? She'd been kidnapped during the summer the previous year. It was now spring. Soon, she would have been gone a year, and her parents would hold a funeral for her.

However, she couldn't go back home. Not yet. Not when there was a good chance that her sisters would be kidnapped next.

By the time they'd finished their meal, night had drawn in around them. The forest had grown still and dark.

Tanelith had hoped that she'd be able to see a clear path up the side of the stairs once the moon touched the rock structure.

However, it looked the same. Large and daunting, an impossible goal.

Vyncis strolled out from under the trees, onto the rocks. "They're still really warm," he commented as he hurried across. He spent some time running his fingers over the rock, then he turned back to Tanelith.

"Didn't you say that the sharp points on the forearms of your armor could be used to climb walls?" he asked.

Tanelith blinked, surprised. "Yes!" she said excitedly. "I didn't think of that."

She pulled out the dagger. Maybe she was imagining it, but it felt to her as if it was eager to transform, to sip at the magic she supplied it and grow long and milky-white.

The rest of the armor formed quickly as well, the glass melting and forming around her.

Tanelith even included the helmet and visor this time. Normally, she didn't bother with it. This time, it just flowed up and over her head before she had a chance to really think about it.

Then she stopped where she was, shock holding her motionless.

A doorway had appeared on the face of the rock structure, highlighted in blue magical light.

Maybe the stairs weren't actually outside the structure, but within it.

THIRTY-SEVEN

When Tanelith lifted the visor, the outline of the doorway disappeared. She could only see it when she was completely encased by the armor.

Maybe it would appear at other times, though. Maybe when the moon was just right, it would highlight the door.

It didn't matter. She might know where to go, now.

Vyncis studied the rock, where Tanelith pointed out the doorway. He shook his head. "I don't see it," he said.

"It's there," Tanelith assured him. "Now, I just have to figure out how to open it."

She quickly crossed over the heated rocks, noting that even in her armor she felt the warmth through the soles of her feet.

Could she, too, use that heat? She had no idea.

There wasn't an obvious door handle on the door. She ran her fingers along the edges, where a handle should be.

Nothing. Then again, her fingers were encased in armor. It was difficult for her to feel anything with them.

Frustrated, she ran her palm along the sides.

Wait. What was that?

It felt like a slight depression in the face of the door, just above where a handle would be.

Tanelith pushed her palm against it.

The door *yielded* to the pressure. It pushed in a little.

Then, to her surprise, the door pushed hard against her palm, springing outward with an audible click.

And opening.

What kind of door did you open by pushing against it? She had no idea what the ancients had been thinking when they'd created such a complicated structure.

Then again, anyone who wasn't being careful, but was just pushing against the door, wouldn't be able to open it.

Tanelith held onto the edge of the door, looking over to catch Vyncis' eye. He stared at her with wide eyes.

Slowly, Tanelith dragged the door back and open.

The air that rushed out smelled so stale that even with her helmet on and her visor down she could still smell it. She took a step back and let the air clear for a moment.

Just inside the threshold was a small room. It had been carved out of the stone itself. The walls of the rock weren't smooth, but had been shaped into natural undulations, as if it had grown there.

It reminded her of Rytha's dwelling.

The space wasn't very large. Perhaps four people could gather in it at the same time.

What took up her attention was the center, where a brilliant light shone down. It was perfectly round.

Dust motes danced in the light. She could see through it to the blank back wall.

That was it, though. No stairs. Just an empty room with a light.

Vyncis came to stand beside her. He looked at her, then back at the room.

"Put your arm in the light," he directed her.

Tanelith crossed the threshold of the room, listening to hear if any alarm bells started ringing. She didn't hear anything though, not any subtle click or even loud gong.

She stuck the arm without the sword into the beam.

Of its own volition, her arm started rising.

Alarmed, she stepped back quickly.

Vyncis nodded. "I think that's your stairs," he told her with a grin.

"I think you're right," she said softly.

Finally, she was here. She could leave Ithlond, and be transported upward...somewhere.

Would there be a city at the other end of that beam?

There was only one way to find out.

THIRTY-EIGHT

Tanelith felt awkward putting her pack on over her armor. But she didn't want to leave it behind.

If there was a city up there, at the end of that beam, she didn't want to just wear the clothes she had on.

She left all the food behind. She hoped she wouldn't need it where she was going. She still kept her water flask with her, just in case.

Vyncis had stayed where he was, holding the door open in case it decided to swing shut. It hadn't, though.

Tanelith came to stand beside him, awkwardly shifting from one foot to the other as the pair of them stared at the mesmerizing beam.

"Are you sure you don't want to come with?" Tanelith asked. She hadn't been pestering him about his decision. She still felt the need to double check.

"No," Vyncis said with a hard shake of his head. He glanced at her. "Don't you feel the heat coming off that?"

Tanelith stuck her face closer to the beam, turning one cheek toward it, then the other. "No," she replied. "If anything, it feels cool. Like moonlight."

"I think that beam is just meant for the Egarlorsar," Vyncis said. "I'd be fried to a crisp if I tried stepping into it."

"I see," Tanelith said. "I'm sorry," she added after a few moments.

"Don't be," Vyncis said. "I wanted to go back home. This just confirms that I made the right decision."

Tanelith nodded, a little sad. "I'm still sorry that we can't continue on together."

He gave her a brave smile. "You'll be off having your own adventures. And so will I. We'll meet again. And you can tell me everything."

"I will," Tanelith said. "I will come and visit you in Gishem Woods. I promise."

"I won't hold you to that," Vyncis said. "I know you might have a war to fight in the meanwhile."

They stood together in silence for a few more moments. Tanelith finally reached out and put her arm across Vyncis' shoulders, giving him a half-hug, the kind she'd give her sisters.

It surprised her when his arms snuck around her waist and he held her tightly, squeezing her awkwardly.

"Goodbye," he said as he released her, stepping back.

"I couldn't have asked for a better guide," Tanelith assured him with tears in her eyes. "Or a better friend."

"I wish I hadn't had to unlearn so much," Vyncis admitted. He rubbed his tears away with the back of his hand. "Gods' speed," he said solemnly.

"May the Goddess look after you, and may the Hidden One keep you safe," Tanelith said.

Vyncis nodded. "I'll stay here for seven nights," he assured her. "In case it doesn't turn out how you think it should, and you need to come back. I'll be happy to guide you back to the inhabited lands."

"Thank you," Tanelith said. "I will try to send you a message if I'm not coming back myself."

They paused again.

"Go on," Vyncis said. "Go step into the beam. I want to watch a legend in the making."

Tanelith shook her head. She was no great hero. But she did as he asked.

Two steps took her across the chamber. Without pausing, she stepped into the center of the beam…

…And immediately started to float up.

"Goodbye! Good luck!" shouted Vyncis from somewhere below her.

She heard a loud click echo in the round chamber. She assumed that when she stepped into the beam, the door had closed and locked itself again.

Up she went. Up and up. The tunnel around her was dark and featureless. She turned her face to look above her, to see what she was approaching.

Were those clouds up there?

Tanelith suddenly felt herself gaining speed. Was she about to be ejected from the top of the stairs? Shot out and into the dark night, only to fall heavily back to the earth?

She tensed, then forcibly made herself loosen up, remembering all of Vyncis' lessons about learning how to fall during a fight.

Though if she fell from the top of the stairs, well, not even his lessons would save her.

Up she went. Further. Faster.

Yes, those were clouds. She shivered as she passed through them, their cold instantly condensing on her armor.

Suddenly, she was above the clouds, soaring across the night sky. But she wasn't falling. No, she continued to rise.

Then she was in clouds again, but these were denser than the first set. She shivered again.

The next thing she knew, solid ground was beneath her feet. She blinked and stepped out, prompted by the armor as much as her own senses.

A mirror stood in front of her.

No, it wasn't a mirror.

It was another person in the full milky-glass armor! She knew it wasn't a mirror because they didn't carry a sword in their hands as she did.

She blinked and looked around.

Where was she?

Fluted white columns rose up around her, supporting an arched ceiling that was the color of the night sky, decorated with golden stars. A fine doorway stood just beyond the guardian, outlined in carved white wood. Beneath her feet, a beautiful mosaic whirled around the round chamber, the green, blue, and gold glittering in the light.

"Who are you? Where am I?" Tanelith said.

The guardian before her hesitated for a brief moment. Then his helmet faded away.

He was clearly an Elf, like her, his pale skin like unsullied clouds, green eyes that glittered like wet grass, long black hair pulled back behind slightly pointed ears.

"I am Mironor. And you have reached the floating city of Vallethlar."

READ MORE!

Be sure to read all of the books in this finished series!
Ruins of the Gods
Stairs of the Gods
Cities of the Gods
Graves of the Gods
Available at your favorite retailers!

ABOUT KNOTTED ROAD PRESS

Knotted Road Press publishes dynamic fiction set in exotic locations and unique non-fiction voices in genres such as autobiography, business, cookbooks, and how-to. Our authors cover a wide range of genres including science fiction, fantasy, mystery, literary, and poetry, appealing to all readers. We offer both DRM-free ebooks and print books for a global readership.

Knotted Road Press
www.KnottedRoadPress.com
www.KnottedRoadPress.com/Shop

www.ingramcontent.com/pod-product-compliance
Lightning Source LLC
Chambersburg PA
CBHW061100100726
47911CB00012B/320